All's Fair In Love

Jeanne Andrews

BANTAM BOOKS
TORONTO · NEW YORK · LONDON · SYDNEY

ALL'S FAIR IN LOVE
A Bantam Book / September 1982

Cover photo by Pat Hill.

Sweet Dreams is a Trademark of Bantam Books, Inc.

All rights reserved.

ISBN 0-553-22607-X

Published simultaneously in the United States and Canada

Bantam Books are published by Bantam Books, Inc. Its trademark,
consisting of the words ''Bantam Books'' and the portrayal of a
rooster, is Registered in U.S. Patent and Trademark Office and in
other countries. Marca Registrada. Bantam Books. Inc., 666 Fifth
Avenue, New York, New York 10103.

PRINTED IN THE UNITED STATES OF AMERICA

O   0 9 8 7 6 5 4 3 2 1

All's Fair In Love

Chapter One

"Dinner's ready, Anne!" Mrs. Jefferson's voice echoed throughout the apartment.

"At last!" Anne sighed, as she rushed into the bathroom to wash up. It had been a long day. The movers had come and gone, leaving mountains of boxes to be organized and unpacked. She'd lost count of how many books she had already arranged on her shelves, dresses she had hung in her closet, and special souvenirs she had tacked to her walls.

She wondered if she would ever get used to living in New York City—it was all so different from the small town in Maine where she had grown up. Even the familiar living-room furniture that had barely filled the rambling old parlor in their Maine house seemed different in the limited space of this new apartment. And her bicycle certainly appeared out of place in the narrow hallway by the door. Now the growling of her stomach was all but drowned out by the honking traffic and all those people scurrying by below her fifth-floor window. Yes, it was different, all right. It was cluttered, new, and noisy, but it was also very exciting. And she had a feeling that living in New York was going to be the best thing that had happened to her in a long time.

She hurried to the dining room and took her place opposite her sister Betty at the table. "Mom, whatever you're cooking smells delicious."

"I can't take credit for the smell or the food," said Mrs. Jefferson, as she placed the cardboard bucket of fried chicken in the middle of the table. "There just wasn't any time to shop or cook, so we'll have to make do for tonight. Dig in." Ann filled her paper plate with chicken and all the trimmings and watched as the rest of her family did the same. She couldn't remember the last time she had eaten off a paper plate. Even when the family had their outdoor barbecues back home, her mother had always used Grandma's old dishes and real silverware. The yard had been crowded with friendly people and there had been enough food to feed an army. Yard. Strange to think of not having a yard anymore.

"Annie, have you heard a single word I've said?" asked her father, bringing her back to the present.

"Sorry, Dad, I guess my mind was wandering."

"Well, then, I'll start over. Your mother and I have already enrolled you and Betty in a fine school. And it's only ten blocks away, so you'll be able to walk. Of course, if it's raining, you can take the bus. All you have to do is walk to Madison Avenue and catch the bus and it will take you right to the entrance of the school."

"Is Madison Avenue the one with the big stores, or the one with the advertising agencies?" Betty asked.

"It's the one with the advertising agencies," replied Mr. Jefferson. "We'll show you the right street and the right bus when the time comes. We still have a week before school starts."

"That will give us some time to buy you girls some new clothes," said Mrs. Jefferson.

"Now you're talking, Mom," said Anne. "Some of those shop windows looked really great. Can we start tomorrow?"

"Hey, you guys," Mr. Jefferson interrupted, grinning, "it's tough enough being the only man in this house and getting a word in edgewise. If you start talking about shopping, I know I'm licked for sure. Could you hold off on buying spree plans long enough for me to tell you about something even more exciting?"

"I don't know what could be more exciting, Dad, but you have five minutes, starting now."

Anne looked down at her watch and counted off the seconds jokingly.

"Come on, Annie, give me a break," Mr. Jefferson said, winking at her. "I have some news that I think you'll be glad to hear."

Now Anne looked up and studied her father's beaming face with curiosity.

"Your mother and I have been asking around to find the best place for you to take gymnastics lessons here in Manhattan, Anne. I think we hit the jackpot. Not only is there a fine club not too far from the apartment, but the coach there has agreed to meet you and see what you can do. His name is Mr. Tompkins, and he's got a great reputation for developing champions. I'm sure he won't mind adding one more to his team. Isn't that great news, Annie?"

"Oh, Dad, I wish you had asked me about this before you went to all the trouble. I'm just not sure that continuing gymnastics here would be such a terrific idea." Anne saw disappointment in her father's eyes and she was sorry.

"What do you mean? Your teacher in Maine said you had a lot of potential. I just assumed that you would want to continue here in New York."

"It's just that there's so much more to do here than there was in Maine. Gymnastics lessons might get in the way."

"Anne, talent is not a thing to be wasted."

Anne had heard that so many times before

that she wanted to scream. Gymnastics was fun but it was not her life, as her father seemed to think. She had started taking gymnastics lessons at a summer camp in Maine about two years ago at the age of fourteen. When her father visited the camp one day and saw her in an exhibition, he was so impressed he persuaded her to continue taking lessons back in town. She didn't mind then, because she needed something to occupy her time during the school year. But two years was enough, and now that she was living in New York, there were plenty of other things to do.

"Maybe I have other talents that haven't been discovered yet, talents that are more interesting and useful," Anne said, hoping to present an argument that would appeal to her father's sense of logic. "If I start taking gymnastics lessons right away, I'll never know what they are."

"Come on, Annie, lighten up. This isn't exactly a life or death decision, you know. I'm sorry if I did the wrong thing, but at least think about it, OK? What have you got to lose? You may find out that you like gymnastics here more than you did in Maine. And, if for some reason you still feel the same way about this later on, you could give it up, no strings. At least see what this club and coach have to offer, all right?"

"Look, honey," Mrs. Jefferson said soothingly, "you're a new girl in a big city. You're excited about all kinds of new things. Your father knows that. But keep in mind that it might be nice to have a place where you really feel you belong. Why not give the gymnastics club a try? At least it will give you a starting point for all your adventures. Besides, your lessons would only be once a week, on Saturday mornings, and that would leave you with plenty of time for all the other things you have in mind."

Anne thought about what her mother had just said, and it seemed to make a lot of sense. A starting point for all her adventures—she liked that.

"While you're considering your mother's advice, consider this, too," Mr. Jefferson said quietly. "The gymnastics club will be a great way to make friends outside of school, friends who have something in common with you."

"You win! You win! I'll give it a try. The two of you on the same side are just too hard to fight. Where is this club and when do I start?"

"Oh, Annie, I'm so glad you're going to do it," Betty said. "Can I come with you on your first day?"

"Oh, sure. And maybe we could do a little shopping afterwards, or stop in a museum, or . . ."

". . . or ride bicycles in the park," said Betty.

"For heaven's sake, Betty, we're in New York now and all you want to do is what you did every Saturday at home," Anne said. "Let's expand our horizons a little, all right?"

There was a moment of silence at the table before everyone burst out laughing. The apartment in New York City was already starting to feel like home, and the whole family was excited about their new life. As Anne walked back to her room, she knew in her heart that everything was going to be all right. In fact, everything was going to more than all right. It was going to be perfect.

Chapter Two

Anne woke up early Saturday morning, threw back her curtains, and smiled as golden rays of sunshine filled her room. It was a lovely day, the kind that made you ready to get going. She searched her closet and dresser, trying to remember where she stashed her new pair of designer jeans and her favorite western cowboy shirts.

"Hey, Annie," Betty said as she barged into the room, "Mom has breakfast on the table and wants to know where you are."

"Well, now that you know where I am, you can tell her I'll be there in a minute. I have to wash up first."

"OK," said Betty, "but you'd better get a move on. Today's the big day, you know, and if you don't hurry, you're going to be late at the club."

"I'll be right there," Anne said as she walked past her sister and into the bathroom. Anne stared at herself in the mirror. Maybe it wouldn't be so bad if she were late. Maybe it would be better if she never showed up for her gymnastics lesson at all. She'd been giving it a lot of thought, and the more she thought about it the more nervous she became. True, her teacher in Maine had said she had promise, but that was Maine and this was New York. What if she made a fool of herself today? What if she weren't really as good as everyone seemed to think? What if the coach refused to accept her, and what if everyone there laughed at her? "Snap out of it," she told her reflection in the mirror. "Things might not be that bad. Give it a chance." She finished washing up, ate a hearty breakfast, and packed her leotard in her tote bag. Then the whole family piled into the elevator and emerged into the bright summer day.

The city was dazzling. Cars, buses, and people came and went in every direction, and Anne couldn't help smiling. She was excited to be a part of it all. As they walked, she began to regain her self-confidence.

She'd always been the type of person who made up her mind about what she wanted and then went after it with everything she had. Back in Maine, she had been at the top of her class at school, had played on the girls' tennis and basketball teams, and had even been pretty popular. Compared to all those achievements, this gymnastics lesson ought to be a piece of cake. It was just for fun, after all.

She stood off to the side as her father questioned the doorman at the entrance of the red-brick building. *You don't have a thing to worry about,* she reassured herself. *The city seems friendly today and the natives will be, too.*

"Anne," her father called, "this is the place." Mr. Jefferson held open the large glass doors and the family filed past him. They took the elevator up to the third floor. There, in front of them, were double doors with the words "Metropolitan Gymnastics Club" stylishly etched on a wide brass plaque. Anne took a deep breath, clutched her bag a little more tightly than usual, opened the doors, and led the way.

Anne had expected a replica of the small, sparse gymnasium in Maine. But when her eyes adjusted to the bright lights, she was startled to see that the gymnastics club took up an entire floor of the building. Directly in front of her were bleachers. To her left was the men's locker room and to her right, the women's locker room. Beyond the bleachers, the room was equipped with all sorts of gymnastics gear: at least five balance beams, three sets of uneven parallel bars, floor exercise mats, vaults, horses, and parallel bars. Sets of leather rings dangled from the ceiling, and sawdust pits were scattered about. It was breathtaking. All the equipment was modern and shiny, the very latest.

And it was a busy scene: teenagers sitting on benches cooling off after a workout; young children walking through balance beam routines, with spotters closely guarding them on either side; men swinging from the rings, and women rehearsing dance exercises on the mats. In the center of all this activity was a man watching a beautiful girl on the uneven parallel bars, barking commands at her in an authoritative voice during her whole performance. Once or twice he made her get off the bars and start from the beginning, urging her to smooth things out or add a move here and there.

"That must be Mr. Tompkins," said her father in a whisper, indicating the man Anne had been watching.

"He sure is hard on that girl," Anne commented, growing afraid that it would soon be her turn. At that instant, Mr. Tompkins noticed them huddled by the door and nodded to them, indicating that he would be right with them. He watched the girl on the bars for a few more seconds, helped her with her dismount, then told her to sit down and rest for a while. "Stay there and think about what you're doing wrong, and we'll start again when I get back." His tone was stern, but before he left her, he threw her a towel and winked at her. "You're getting there," he said slyly.

"You must be the Jeffersons," said Mr. Tompkins as he approached. "It's a pleasure to meet you all." He extended his hand to Anne's parents, gave Betty a broad smile, and placed his arm around Anne's shoulders. "And you must be Anne. I've heard a lot about you. Why don't we go into my office and have a chat. I'd like to know a little more about your background."

They followed Mr. Tompkins to a glass cubicle at the far end of the room. Once inside, he closed the door and they all took seats around the small wooden desk.

"Now, Anne, your father tells me that you've been studying gymnastics for about two years now."

"Yes, sir, but I'm not sure I could keep up with some of the performances I've seen here today." She was angry at herself for starting the interview off with excuses, but she was afraid that her father might have exaggerated her abilities.

"Don't worry about that. Let me be the judge. Keep in mind that we have all types of students in this club. Some come here for exercise, others for fun, and still others because they hope to be serious contenders in the amateur gymnastics field."

Anne looked over at her father. She knew he wanted her to say that she was serious, but that would have been misleading and she would

12

be getting in over her head. "Honestly, Mr. Tompkins," Anne faltered, "I believe that, right now, I fall into the fun category." Out of the corner of her eye, she saw her father shift in his chair. "But that could change," she added quickly. "You see, I'm just not sure yet if I have the potential to become a serious competitor."

"Well, that's fair enough," Mr. Tompkins nodded. "Why don't we find out right away what you do have. Have you brought a workout suit with you?"

"Yes, sir."

"Good. Then, why don't you go change and we'll see what you can do. Would you like to start with the uneven parallel bars?"

"That would be fine," Anne said timidly. She thought about the girl she had been watching earlier and knew hers would be a tough act to follow.

"Great, then. I'll meet you there. Mr. Jefferson, would you and the rest of your family follow me? I'll find you some front-row seats."

Anne watched her family zigzag their way across the crowded floor to a row of benches beside the parallel bars. She picked up her bag and went into the locker room to change. She hung her clothes up on a rack filled with hangers and stowed her tote bag below. Then she took her brush and elastic band over to the mirror and pulled her hair back and out of the way. She gave herself one long, critical look in the full-length mirror, decided she was as ready as she would ever be, raised her head proudly, and returned to the gym.

Mr. Tompkins was working with the same young woman as he had been before, and Anne took a seat on the sidelines and watched. The girl was amazing. She made even the most difficult moves seem easy as she spun and twirled and floated around the wooden bars. Her routine was absolutely perfect.

Anne noticed that she was not the only one watching. Sitting a few feet away from her was a boy about her age, maybe a little older. Her eyes opened wider as she got a good look at him. He was gorgeous. Although he was sitting hunched over, Anne could tell that he was tall and lean and strong. His hair was honey-colored and covered his ears. As he watched the routine, his face became intense, and his blue eyes sparkled.

Then she watched him suddenly get up and walk over to a practice mat in the middle of the floor. A small girl, not more than nine or ten years old, was working out there without a spotter. He stayed on the edge of the mat, apparently not wanting to intrude, but watching the child protectively. The little girl flipped in midair and came crashing down on the mat. Anne watched, entranced, as the boy ran over to the girl, scooped her off the mat, and cradled her in his arms. When he was sure she was all right, he pretended to be very stern.

"What are you doing working out without a spotter? You could have hurt yourself and ruined your chances in the 1988 Olympics."

The girl whined, "I'll never get to the Olympics. I can never get that tumbling part right."

"Why don't you do it for me, and I'll try to see what's going wrong."

The little girl looked into his eyes, flattered that he was willing to show her so much attention. "Would you? Really?"

"Sure. Go ahead." The little girl took her place on the other side of the mat and began her series of tumbles from the beginning. As soon as she came to the difficult move, she fell flat on her back again. "See?" she moaned, tears streaming down both cheeks.

"Nothing to it, kid," he said, drying her eyes. "You're just starting your takeoff from the wrong foot. Now, try it again, and when you get to the cartwheel, make sure you land on your left leg, so you can take off for the somersaults on your right. Do it slowly this time, OK?"

"OK," she said, relieved that her problem was so simple. She started one more time and, finally, completed the series of moves perfectly. "Wow, you were right. Thanks a lot."

He walked over to her and put his arm around her. "You're very good," he said, "but will you promise me that you won't ever work by yourself again? If I have to worry about you getting hurt, I won't be able to concentrate on my own routines."

The little girl smiled up at him. "I promise," she said shyly. "Will you help me some more later?"

"You bet. But I have to go now, so find yourself another spotter for a while. I'll be back to check you out after my lesson, OK?"

"OK."

Anne was really impressed. There weren't many guys around who would take the time to help a little kid like that. There also weren't many guys around who could be so patient and understanding. He was special, all right. He had charmed that little girl, and he had charmed Anne, too. She couldn't take her eyes off him, and she just knew that he would be great to be with.

"Not bad, huh?" whispered Betty, as she sneaked up behind Anne.

"Yeah, she's really good," replied Anne.

"I wasn't talking about her, I was talking about him, and don't pretend you don't know what I'm talking about."

"He's OK, Betty, but I'm trying to concentrate on the things Mr. Tompkins is looking for. Now leave me alone or I'll blow it." As Betty inched away, Anne took one last furtive look at the boy behind her. Not bad at all. Then, she focused her attention on the last part of the lesson in progress. The girl made a few wide circles around the bar, dismounted, and walked over to the bench to sit down. "Good job," said Mr. Tompkins, sitting beside her. "Maybe we'll try that bar-release move next week." Mr. Tompkins turned to Anne. "Ready?"

Anne walked over to the bar. "I'll spot for you," Mr. Tompkins said, lifting her up to the higher bar. Anne felt as if everyone in the room had stopped what they were doing to examine the new kid on the block. Her stomach was fluttering as she went through the moves she had practiced so often, trying as hard as she could to perform each one perfectly. After a few moments she relaxed and began to enjoy herself. Her body obeyed every command she gave it, and she felt almost as if she were flying. When she landed on the ground, she stood tall and proud, knowing that she had done her best and that she had been good.

"Wow! That was really something," Mr. Tompkins said. He put his hands on her shoulders and gave her a friendly shake. "You really had me fooled with that little speech of yours earlier. After seeing you move, I'd be very happy to give you lessons and continue your training."

Training? Had she heard him correctly? She had done well and was pleased with herself, but training was serious and she had meant what she said in her "little speech" about being there for fun.

Mr. Jefferson came over to join the conversation. "What do you think?" he asked Mr. Tompkins.

"I was just telling Anne that I would be happy to have her join the club. Her teacher in Maine wasn't exaggerating when she said that your daughter had a lot of promise. With the right type of exercises, she could be as good as the best of them."

Mr. Jefferson beamed. "Are there any forms that have to be filled out? Shall we discuss the fee?"

Anne's father and her new coach walked back into the glass cubicle without even consulting Anne about her wishes. She grabbed a towel and sat down on the bench, desperately trying to hold back her tears. As she wiped the sweat from her face and brushed back the few strands of hair wilting across her forehead, Betty and her mother approached her.

"Anne, I'm so proud of you," her mother said, embracing her.

"Annie, you were great," said Betty. "And I wasn't the only one who thought so. Mr. Wonderful over there never took his baby blues off you."

Anne had forgotten about the guy in the fourth row. She turned her head around slowly and was embarrassed when she found herself staring right into his eyes. He smiled at her and gave her the thumbs-up sign before she snapped her head back to her sister. Although Betty and Mrs. Jefferson continued talking, Anne didn't hear a word. The only thing she heard was her heart pounding inside her and rockets going off in her head. Her body became warm and tingling all over, and a shiver ran up her spine. Nothing had ever affected her this way before. She wished he would come down and talk to her, but it never happened. Instead, her father returned and told her that everything was all set and that she should hurry up and change so they could all grab a bite to eat and do some sightseeing.

Anne had to force herself to move. She struggled into the locker room and collapsed into a chair. When she happened to glance into the mirror, she let out a gasp. She looked awful. Why hadn't he noticed her when she first came into the club looking fresh and fashionably dressed in her new clothes? Why did he have to look at her now, after a workout, drenched with sweat, a real mess? Now Anne was up and rushing around. Maybe if she hurried, she would be able to get herself into shape and back out to the gym before he left. She showered, changed, and combed her hair.

She burst through the locker room door and ran across the crowded floor. She scanned the bleachers rapidly, but he was gone. As her parents moved her towards the door, Anne looked into every corner of the gym, hoping to catch sight of him again. No luck. Well, there was always next week. Anne had never looked forward to anything the way she now looked forward to seeing that boy again. She had forgotten all about her worries that the club might take up too much of her time.

"You know, Dad," she said, raising her voice to be heard over the traffic rumbling past them on the street, "I think this gymnastics club was the best idea you've had in a long time."

"I'm so glad you're so happy about it," said Mr. Jefferson, surprised at her enthusiasm.

Anne looked over at Betty, and the two sisters gave each other a knowing wink.

Chapter Three

The first week of school passed quickly for Anne. She and Betty walked there early Monday morning, registered for classes, and reported to their homerooms. Anne was amazed at how many extra-curricular activities the school offered. But none of them seemed to appeal to her, and she knew why. She could hardly wait for Saturday to come around, the day she would be able to return to the gymnastics club and see her mystery man again.

As she thought about how great it would be to have a boyfriend again, her thoughts went back to Steve. The mere thought of his name brought back vivid memories. She was transported back to a large, rambling high school in Maine, very different from the small brick building through which she was now walking. Her old high school was spread out over acres of pine-covered land. A high stone wall surrounded the campus. Inside, the halls were wide and covered with bulletin boards. Anne used to stop along those halls, reading announcements, talking to friends, gossiping, discussing who was dating whom and where the party would be held after the next big game. She used to linger in the halls, hoping to run into Steve, the most popular boy at school and her steady date.

Anne and Steve had been the talk of the school. Most of Anne's friends agreed that they made the perfect couple. They looked right together, they had the same interests, and they were both top students. Everyone thought they would stay together forever. So did Anne. There was no denying that Steve made her feel special.

He was the star pitcher of the baseball team and led the league in runs batted in. He was in his junior year and already had received many scholarship offers from some of the finest schools in the country. Most important of all, though, was the way he cared about Anne and never took her for granted.

It had been a storybook romance until Anne told him about her father's promotion and their upcoming move. Then, everything changed. Their sweet relationship soured in the course of a week. Anne had seen it coming and could understand what was happening.

Steve was the big man on campus. He didn't want to spend his last year at Brunswick High School writing letters to a girlfriend in New

York. He needed a new one and fast. His reputation depended on it. Oh, it was easy to understand, but not so easy to take. Steve continued to be friendly; he even bought her a going-away present. But he also asked for his ring back and started dating Alice Parker, even before the moving van had arrived.

All of Anne's friends had been sympathetic. They had given her a huge going-away party and had promised to write and visit. They were very supportive, but it didn't help. Anne remembered walking through those wide halls for the last time, kissing friends goodbye, reading announcements for the coming year, and feeling sorry that she wouldn't be there to participate. She had seen Steve and Alice Parker walking hand in hand and had fought off the urge to cry. She had vowed then that her life in New York would be every bit as special as her life in Maine had been. She would make new friends and she would be even more popular than she had been before. She would show them all, especially Steve. And she would show herself that she could do it.

What would her old friends think of the mysterious stranger at the Metropolitan Gymnastics Club? Would he stack up to Steve? Yes, definitely yes. It was settled then. She would let him make her forget Steve. She would let him make her feel special again.

When Saturday finally arrived, Anne woke

up early to wash her hair and select the right outfit. She laid out her gym clothes with special care and made sure that there was not a single spot on them. As soon as she had gobbled down her breakfast, she left.

As she approached the entrance to the Metropolitan Gymnastics Club, a feeling of expectation ran through her, then a sharp pang of fear. She took a deep breath and walked in.

Things were as hectic as they had been the week before. Everyone was hard at work. The intensive activity stirred Anne and made her want to become a part of it all. As she made her way to the locker room, she scanned the floor of the club and there, on the nearest set of rings, was her mystery man.

She felt as if a thousand butterflies had been let loose in her stomach. She stumbled into the locker room and changed her clothes, feeling happier than she could ever remember feeling. She couldn't explain this giddiness to herself. She had met boys before, had gone out on dates before, but she had never felt anything like this before.

Maybe she was being childish, building up something in her mind perhaps more out of fantasy than reality. After all, she hadn't even been introduced to him. He might have a girlfriend already. He might not be her type. Still, there was something about the way he had looked at her that brought chills to her body, that had caused her imagination to race out of control, that had created an overpowering need to meet him. Anne was still deep in thought as she entered the gym, and it was the sound of her name from a distance that brought her back from her daydreaming.

"Miss Jefferson, over here."

It was the coach's voice, calling to her from the middle of the room. She spotted him and raced over to him. "Good morning, Mr. Tompkins," she said. "I hope I'm not too late."

"As a matter of fact, you're a little early. I still have one lesson to give before yours. Why don't you work out a bit on one of the mats while you're waiting. That way, you'll be warmed up and ready to go by the time I finish here. Let me find you a spotter, OK?"

"Sure," Anne replied, feeling a little embarrassed that the coach thought she would need a spotter just to warm up. As Anne did some preliminary bending and stretching exercises, she noticed Mr. Tompkins motioning to someone across the room. Moments later that someone came loping over.

"Anne, I'd like you to meet Greg Bartos. Greg, this is Anne Jefferson." Anne looked up to see who had been appointed her babysitter. She almost dropped to the floor when she realized that her mystery man was standing right beside her, smiling and extending his hand to her.

"It's very nice to meet you, Anne. I saw you working out last week and I was very impressed."

"Thank you, Greg," was all she managed to say.

"Greg, would you mind spotting for Anne while I give Sarah her lesson?" Mr. Tompkins asked, already certain of the answer.

"Not at all. Shall we?"

Anne followed Greg to one of the vacant mats in the center of the gym. She dusted a little of the snowy chalk on her hands and feet and continued to limber up. She couldn't think of anything brilliant to say and so decided to say nothing. Finally, Greg broke the ice. "Do you have a floor exercise routine that you've done before?"

"Yes, I do, but it's a little dull."

"Well, why not start with that. Maybe later we could add a few moves to perk it up a bit."

"OK," Anne said. "The only time I really need a spotter is on the first series of somersaults. I do a double with a twist on the first turn."

Greg smiled at her. "I'm sure you don't need a spotter at all, but it's club rules, insurance and all that."

Anne went through her exercise without a hitch. Although she had never performed it without music before, her body seemed attuned to the rhythm of her pounding heart. When she was finished, Greg came over and patted her on the back. "That was really great," he said. "You could do a lot with that format to make it more difficult, if you wanted. Let me show you what I mean." As Greg demonstrated some tumbling moves and suggested where they might be added for effect, Anne was stunned. Not only was he extremely handsome, but talented as well. She watched him do flips and splits and was really impressed.

"You're very good," she said when he had finished his demonstration.

"Not as good as I'd like to be," he replied, "but I love it."

"How did you get into gymnastics?"

"I discovered it through my sister," Greg said, nodding over at the uneven parallel bars. "That girl is my sister Sarah."

Anne looked over and saw the same attractive girl who had preceded her the week before. She couldn't hide her smile of relief. At least it wasn't his girlfriend. She felt a lot more at ease now, and the rest of her workout with Greg sped by. Every move he showed her, she was able to copy precisely. Before they had finished, she had incorporated them all into her original routine.

"You really learn fast," he said, sitting beside her on the bench. "I think you're already doing those moves better than I ever could. Either I'm a great teacher or you're an incredibly fast learner."

Anne felt a flush of embarrassment and gave a little laugh. "Oh, it was probably just beginner's luck."

"No way," he insisted. "You really shouldn't put yourself down that way," he said, becoming very serious. "You could be a very strong competitor with your skills. All you need now is the right kind of attitude."

Anne hesitated. This did not seem the right time to tell Greg that she had no intention of ever becoming a competitor. Before she could decide what to say, Greg continued. "My sister is a perfect example of the right kind of attitude. I believe she's one of the finest gymnasts in the United States today. She has everything she needs technically, and more important, mentally. She was a winner from the day she was born."

"That must be an awfully hard act to follow," Anne said, trying to sound sympathetic.

"But I don't try to follow her act. I've learned from it and occasionally try to imitate it, but on the whole I just sit back and respect it and admire it. From as far back as I can remember, my father has been telling us to go after anything we wanted and that if we wanted it badly enough, it would be ours. He called that his winning attitude."

"I've always felt that way, too," Anne said, trying to attract some of Greg's attention back to herself.

"Well, Sarah's really made his words come alive. She's put everything my parents taught us into practice."

Anne was becoming a little annoyed. All he wanted to talk about was his sister. But she didn't want him to know that she was bored, so she tried to sound as interested as possible.

"Has your sister been in a lot of competitions?"

"Has she ever!" Greg answered, turning to face her. "At first Coach Tompkins was reluctant to let her enter anything. He wasn't sure she was ready. But once he let her participate in her first meet, there was no stopping her. As a matter of fact, I can't remember one single competition in which Sarah didn't place in the top three, including that first big one."

"That's very impressive," Anne said, trying to be polite.

"Dad has even joked about turning our den into a trophy room for Sarah. She has dozens of medals and plaques and statues that she won in competitions. I have a feeling that she just might make it to the Olympic Games. Coach Tompkins has hinted as much to her."

"Wow," Anne said, trying to stifle the anger that was building up inside of her. She glanced over at Sarah, who was working tirelessly to perfect every little movement in her routine. She wished Sarah would finish so she could get started. This conversation with Greg was frustrating. She had absolutely nothing to say, and when she could get a word in, Greg paid no attention. Anne could feel herself drooping and her spirits sagging. She knew something had to be done quickly to change things.

As she focused her attention on Sarah, she secretly hoped that Greg's sister would make one mistake, just a small one, to prove to her worshipping brother that she was truly human. It was almost as if Sarah had picked up Anne's hostile waves, for at that very moment, she slipped off the top bar and landed on her bottom on the mat. Coach Tompkins shook his head and scolded her about her lack of concentration.

Anne couldn't help feeling terribly guilty. While she knew the slip was not her fault, she was troubled that Sarah could arouse such negative feelings in her. Anne always had been able to get along with people. Yet here she sat, watching Sarah, envying Sarah, and disliking Sarah without ever having met her. Anne was really confused. She needed time to sort things out, to calm herself, to adapt to the conflicting emotions she was experiencing. She was glad when Coach Tompkins finally called her over to the bars to begin her lesson.

As she chalked up her hands to keep from slipping, she tried to clear her mind of the million crazy thoughts buzzing around inside it. She sat up on the high bar and listened to the coach's instructions. *Calm down and concentrate,* she told herself over and over. She began her practice, letting her body glide freely, letting the snapping and creaking of the bars push out all the bad feelings and replace them with a sort of peaceful calm. As her mind began to clear, Anne began to feel better. She worked for more than half an hour, listening to the coach's instructions and following them to the letter. During that time, nothing else mattered, no other voices were heard, and no other problems were allowed to creep in. Once again, Anne's routine went well, and she was pleased with herself when her lesson came to an end. The coach complimented her on her ability to learn quickly and said that he would like to see her on some of the other apparatus next week.

"If you can vault as well as you swing, you could be ready for a small meet very soon."

"Coach," Anne said quietly, "I really meant what I told you last week about being here for fun. I don't think I'm ready for a meet, no matter how small, and I'm not sure I'll ever want to be ready. I hope that what I'm saying doesn't disappoint you or make you think less highly of me, but I really am here for the fun of gymnastics without any of the pressures."

"I understand, Anne," Mr. Tompkins said, a combination of warmth and disappointment in his voice. "I only thought that once you realized your potential your attitude would change.

I'm not trying to push you into anything you don't want, and I certainly don't think any less of you because of it. On the contrary, I respect your honesty. However, I owe it to my serious students to spend more time with them. I'd be happy to continue to give you lessons every week, but they'll have to be a little shorter. Is that all right with you?"

"That's fine, sir."

"And, Anne," Mr. Tomkins continued hopefully, "if you ever change your mind about competition, let me be the first to know, will you?"

"You can count on that."

"Good, then I'll see you next week. Bye."

Anne walked slowly over to the bench where she and Greg had been sitting. She collapsed there, wiping herself with her towel, trying to cool off. As soon as she regained her energy, she collected her gear and wandered into the locker room.

She stood under the shower for a long time. She leaned against the tiled wall, letting the cool water cascade over her body and clear her head. It had been some long morning. Anne couldn't remember ever being so mentally and physically exhausted. Where had things gone wrong? The day had started off perfectly. She had gotten to meet Greg right away, and she had been able to spend most of the morning with him, getting to know him. What had happened? How had she managed to lose control?

It all came down to Sarah. In less than two hours, Greg's sister had become her enemy, even though they'd never met. The more Anne thought about the events of the day, the more she believed that Sarah was the problem. How could Greg ever be really interested in someone as ordinary as Anne? He'd always be comparing her to Sarah. And Anne would never be good enough to meet his standards.

As she was about to leave the gym, she took one final look around. There were Greg and Sarah. They were sitting on a bench going over Sarah's routine one more time. Anne sighed. Just as she turned away, Greg looked up and saw her. "See you next week, champ," he shouted. Then he smiled. That did it. Whatever the obstacles, whatever the problems, Anne knew that she had to give this friendship a chance. It might take a little planning and a little time, but she would find a way to open his eyes.

Chapter Four

The next week was an especially good one for Anne. She got an A on her first English theme and a B-plus on her first math quiz. A girl at school invited her to a party where everyone tried to make her feel part of the group. And her class went on a field trip to the Metropolitan Museum of Art, which Anne loved.

Later in the week, her father came home with four tickets to the theater, and the entire family went to see a Broadway musical hit. Anne was beginning to feel that she really belonged in New York City. It felt like home now, and she decided there was no other place in the world she'd rather live.

By Saturday she was feeling so good that she even looked forward to gymnastics class again. Gone were the doubts and annoyances of the week before. All she remembered was the thrill of performing her routine . . . and the excitement of Greg's smile.

She found a secluded corner of the gym and began to warm up. She stretched her muscles and limbered them. She did splits, backbends, and handstands. And all the while, of course, she was on the lookout for Greg. As her body began to relax and rid itself of the kinks, she heard a familiar voice behind her.

"Trying to avoid me this morning?" Greg asked.

"Huh?" Anne snapped around, a quizzical expression on her face.

"Why else would you be warming up way over here?" Greg laughed and Anne joined in. It felt good to know that he had been looking for her.

"Honestly, Greg, I wasn't trying to avoid you. I just felt a little groggy this morning and needed the privacy to wake myself up before facing the coach."

"Well, I'll leave you alone then," he said, and he turned to walk away."

"No!" Anne cried, a little too loudly and forcefully. "I mean . . . I'm finished anyway."

She walked over with him to the bleachers and sat down to watch the various activities going on around them. Neither of them spoke a word for a while. Then, finally, Greg broke the silence. "So, where are you from, Anne?"

35

"I'm originally from Brunswick, Maine. We came to live in New York when my father's company opened an office here and assigned him to run it. It's a big promotion for him, and we're all really excited about it."

"Do you have any brothers or sisters?"

"I have a younger sister, Betty. She's fifteen. We get along pretty well for sisters, I guess."

"How do you like the big, bad city?"

"I love it!" Anne said, her eyes lighting with excitement. "It really is the greatest city in the world . . . not that I've seen many others, of course. At first I was a little scared of all the changes, but now I'm glad we moved. Maine is pretty, but nothing can compare with the thrill of walking down Fifth Avenue."

Anne stopped momentarily to catch her breath. Her words had come pouring out, and now she felt a little embarrassed. *Greg must think I sound like a real hick*, she thought. She glanced up at him, afraid he'd look bored, but he was smiling at her, waiting for her to go on. "There's just so much to see and do here that sometimes it makes my head spin," she said laughingly.

"It sounds to me like you need a tour guide. I'd be happy to offer my services sometime. I'd like to show you some of the city that isn't on the standard tourist map. I think you'd really get a kick out of it. I know I still do."

"That sounds like fun," Anne replied.

Another spark of hope! She was getting warm already.

"What sounds like fun?" Suddenly Sarah Bartos was standing right there beside them.

"Hey Sarah, I want you to meet a new member of the club. Anne, this is my sister Sarah."

"It's a pleasure to meet you, Anne. Greg has told me a lot about you."

Anne knew Sarah was only trying to be polite. What could Greg possibly have known about her to tell Sarah? *Give her a chance,* Anne warned herself. *Don't let your first impressions get in the way of a possible friendship. Loosen up.*

"It's nice to meet you, too, Sarah. Greg has told me a lot about you, and I really do admire your talents." That was easy—and all true.

"You're not so bad yourself, kid," Sarah said. Although Sarah's use of the word "kid" made Anne's skin crawl, she smiled up at Greg's older sister and said nothing.

"Anne was just telling me about her discovery of New York. She's from out of town, you know, and has started to explore a little on her own." Greg sounded proud, as if Anne's sightseeing was quite an accomplishment.

"That's wonderful," Sarah said. "Where have you been?"

Was she really interested, or was she just humoring her brother's little friend? Anne could

37

not be sure, but she decided to give Sarah a chance.

"As a matter of fact," Anne began, trying to sound casual, "last night we went to see a Broadway show, that new musical at the Lunt-Fontanne Theatre. It was wonderful. We sat in the fourth row center and had a perfect view of everything. I thought the acting was great and the sets were really incredible. The first act was dynamite, and by the end of the play my hands were limp from applauding. Have you seen the show?" Anne asked.

"Oh, yes," Sarah said, matching Anne's enthusiasm. "As a matter of fact, a good friend of mine is in the cast. She plays the younger sister. The night the show opened she invited me to sit backstage, to give her moral support and all that. I must say, watching a play from backstage is the most exciting thing in the world. You get a real feel for the behind-the-scenes atmosphere. Anyway, after the play was over, we all went to Sardi's to wait for the reviews. It's sort of a tradition in the theater. My friend couldn't relax and enjoy the cast party until she saw the raves in all the papers. What a night! I think I told you about that party, didn't I, Greg? It was the one where Paul Newman stopped by to congratulate everybody."

Greg told his sister that he remembered the story well, and they started reminiscing about that night. All the while Anne just sat there, looking attentive but not hearing a word. Her bubble had been burst, and she felt like crying. Sarah had taken one of the most exciting evenings of Anne's life and turned it into nothing. Furthermore, she had captured Greg's attention and had engaged him in a conversation about which Anne knew nothing and in which she could not participate. And Greg was too deep in conversation to even notice Anne's reaction. *It's funny,* she thought. *I was relieved when I found out that Sarah was Greg's sister. But she keeps coming between Greg and me anyway.*

"Well, well, well. One would think, looking at the three of you, that this was a social club and not a gymnastics club," Mr. Tompkins said with a chuckle. "I suppose all of you think you're good enough not to need today's lessons. That's OK with me. There are other fish in the sea," he said and started to walk away.

"Come on back here, Coach," Sarah said with a twinkle in her eye. "You know the best fishing is right here."

Mr. Tompkins returned and sat down beside them. "As a matter of fact, I'm glad you're all here." Anne felt sure he would have been just as happy if she had been absent. He was obviously talking mainly to Greg and Sarah. "We just set the date for the annual club championship. It begins three months from today. I have the sign-up sheets right here. Anyone in this group care to put their John Hancocks on the dotted line?"

"I wouldn't miss this for the world!" Sarah exclaimed, grabbing the pen out of Mr. Tompkins's hand. Greg signed the sheet next, and then all eyes were on Anne. She felt her body stiffen. She felt conspicuous and uncomfortable. "How about it, Anne? Would you like to sign up?" Sarah handed her the sheet.

Anne hesitated. "I—I really don't know anything about the competition," she stammered, trying to buy herself a little time to think of a good reason not to sign the sheet.

"Well, let me explain," Coach Tompkins said, realizing the pressure his new student must be feeling. "Every year, the club holds a championship among the members. It's a pretty well-known competition in the gymnastics world because, as you know, this club has a good reputation. We hold the men's tournament on Saturday and the women's on Sunday, followed by a formal ball at the Plaza Hotel. Medals are awarded to the top-scoring competitors in each of the individual events. An enormous gold medal goes to the all-around champion, the second-place winner gets a silver medal, and third place wins a bronze. Sometimes our competition even makes the sports page."

"We made it last year," Greg said. "Sarah got her name in print. She won the all-around competition and three out of the four individual events."

"Sarah has won the competition for the last four years in a row," the coach added. "We sure could use someone to give her a run for the money. How about it, Anne?"

Again, all eyes were on Anne, as Mr. Tompkins and Greg and Sarah waited to hear the verdict. Anne put her mind into fifth gear and sent the pros and cons zooming around in her head. First she looked at the coach. He knew she didn't want to compete, yet he had made a point of including her in the group. Why? Did he really think she could defeat Sarah? Or was he just trying to stir up a little rivalry?

Then she turned to Greg's sister. Sarah was the champion, so smug, so sure of herself, so confident of another victory. How satisfying it would be to teach her a lesson in humility. But what if Anne never came close? Then she'd only make a fool of herself and make Sarah look that much better to everyone around.

Finally, Anne stared right into Greg's eyes. They were so clear and blue that she hoped to somehow find the answer she needed there. And find it she did. Here was a chance to prove to Greg that she was as good as his sister. Yes, she thought, the perfect way to win Greg's attention and admiration was to beat Sarah at her own game. Anne took the sheet from Sarah and, trying to steady her trembling hand, signed her name below Greg's.

"Good for you, Anne," said Mr. Tompkins. "Now if you want to have a chance at winning the gold, you had better get off the floor and over to the vault." The coach put his arm around Anne as he walked her over to the apparatus. "I guess you've given more thought to what we talked about last week, and this is your way of telling me that you've decided to become serious, right?"

"I have never been more serious about anything in my life," Anne said. "And I hope you'll be able to give me enough of your time to get me ready for the tournament. I'm determined to win the gold medal."

"I'll do whatever I can to help you. Just be careful that you don't set yourself up for a fall or make your goals unrealistically high. You're good, but you don't have as much experience as some of our other members."

"You're talking about Sarah, aren't you?"

"Sarah, among others. Anne, you've had a few years of on-again, off-again lessons. You've never really been in a competition, and even though ours is open only to the members of the club, it's going to be a tough place to start. Are you sure you're ready for this?"

Anne hesitated. "Why did you encourage me to sign up if you didn't think I had a chance in the first place?" she asked, bewildered.

"I never said that I didn't think you had a chance. I think you'll make a fine showing. I just don't want you to expect too much of yourself too soon. You might be disappointed."

"I won't be disappointed. I'm going to win."

The sound of her final words to the coach echoed in her brain for the rest of the day. *I'm going to win.* She had said it and she meant it. She had set herself a goal and was going to achieve it. She imagined herself standing in the spotlight as Mr. Tompkins delicately placed the gold medal around her neck. She could hear the roar of the crowd as the underdog took the spotlight away from the former champion. She could see Greg beaming in front of her and Sarah crouching, exhausted, in the corner. . . . *I'm going to win.* She had set tough goals for herself in the past and reached them. Just because this goal was a little harder and higher didn't mean that it was impossible to reach.

Anne paid close attention to every word Mr. Tompkins said that morning. She went through the pikes, the twists, the dismounts and the landings over and over again until she had gotten each one of them down to a science. She worked effortlessly on the vault and the balance beam for over an hour, and after her lesson was over, she went off by herself to practice the additions to her floor exercise that Greg had suggested the week before. When she finally grabbed her towel and sat down to rest, she was amazed at how good she felt. She had a purpose now, something to shoot for. It made her time at the club speed by. She was doing the right thing—she knew that now—and it felt good to be running *toward* something instead of running away.

"I've never seen so much energy come from one person in my life," Greg said, coming over after he had finished his lesson. He was already dressed and ready to leave. Anne gave him a quick smile. He looked super, as usual. "Do you think you have enough energy left to make it to the locker room?" he asked. "The gym is about to close for the day."

Anne looked over at the clock on the wall. "Oh, no, I had no idea it was so late. My mother has probably called the police by now."

"There's a phone in Mr. Tompkins's office. Why don't you give her a call and let her know that you're on your way? Or better yet, you could tell her you'll be even later and come have a Coke with me."

"Thanks, I'd like that," Anne said with a smile.

"Well, I'll see you in a few minutes, then, after you've changed."

"You bet," Anne said. A few minutes? *A few hours wold be more like it,* Anne thought. In a happy panic she raced around the locker room, trying to make herself presentable after her long workout.

44

After they had walked to the coffee shop across the street, sat down in a booth and ordered sodas, Anne started worrying. Would they have anything left to say to each other now? Why were her hands shaking? Oh, it was going to be very impressive when she picked up her glass and spilled her drink all over herself.

"Anne," Greg said, "tell me some more about Maine. I've always wanted to travel through New England but never had the chance."

"It's beautiful country up there. There are gorgeous wooded mountains and sparkling blue lakes, and the smell from the pine trees just about surrounds you wherever you go. The summers are sunny and warm, and the winters are snowy and white, but spring and fall are my favorites. That's when all the colors burst out and make you feel as if you're in the middle of an enormous oil painting." Anne paused, noticing the faraway look in Greg's eyes. "You've offered to be my tour guide in New York. Maybe I could return the favor if you ever go up to Maine."

"You've got a deal," Greg said, taking a sip of his soda.

"Have you traveled a lot?" Anne asked.

"Not as much as I'd like to. My parents take me with them whenever they can. Two years ago, I went back to Hungary with them. That had to be the most exciting trip of my life. My parents grew up in Hungary. They didn't come to the United States until the nineteen-fifties. It is still a beautiful country, and I think that made it harder for them, in a way, to go back. I couldn't help but wonder what I would have been like, how different I would be now, if my parents hadn't come here. I was very affected by the whole experience."

"In what way?"

"Well, as soon as I got back to the States, I started reading everything I could get my hands on about the country and its people. I sat my parents down and made them list their ancestors as far back as they could remember. I drew a family tree for myself and wrote short biographies about all the relatives I had met back in the old country. I guess this sounds silly to you, but it was important to me to find out where my family came from, where I belonged. Weird, huh?"

"No, I think it's fascinating. I probably would have done the same thing myself. As a matter of fact, I started tracing my family back once, a long time ago. It started as a school project, but I got so interested I couldn't stop."

"Has your family been in the United States a long time?"

"Yup. I think I could trace my family back to one of the groups of original colonists."

"Why aren't you sure?"

"Promise not to laugh?"

"I promise."

"Well, I started going back past my great-grandparents and I discovered that their parents were originally from Salem, Massachusetts. I was afraid I would discover that I had a witch in my family, and I wasn't ready for that." Anne giggled and made a face.

"My great-uncle was a gypsy horse thief," Greg said. Anne couldn't tell if he was kidding or not until he smiled, then laughed. "Seriously, though, I think roots and family trees are important. When you live with a lot of love around you, you want to spread it around. Do you know what I mean?"

"Yes," Anne responded, too swept up to say any more. She honestly was moved by Greg's words. And besides, maybe, if she was lucky, Greg would spread some of that love to her!

After that, she couldn't take her eyes off him. He was so special. In less than half an hour he had managed to make her relax, make her feel that she had a lot in common with him, make her feel his equal, his friend. Anne was certain, now more than ever, that she wanted more than that.

As they parted on the street corner after promising to get together again the following week after their lessons, Anne was full of happiness and pride. She wondered what it would be like to be Greg's girlfriend, to have him all to herself for an evening without the distractions of the gymnastics club. How would it feel to hold his hand, to sit next to him in a movie, to spend hours on the phone listening to his voice?

The city was incredibly sunny, almost as bright as her mood, as she drifted home that afternoon. With every step her confidence grew. *I am going to win. I am going to win that gold medal, and I am going to win Greg.* She had never failed before, and she was not going to fail this time.

Chapter Five

Anne tiptoed around her small bedroom, trying to focus her eyes in the dark. It was six o'clock Sunday morning, and Anne knew that waking Betty this early would mean trouble. Nothing was where it was supposed to be. She had to open twice as many drawers as she had planned in order to find her sweatsuit and running shoes, and every time a drawer creaked, Betty would roll over in her bed and moan and Anne would freeze in her tracks.

She decided to feel her way out of the bedroom and into the bathroom where she could at least turn on a light and make a little noise without giving herself away. She smiled as she twisted her hair into a knot in the back of her head and fastened it with a large barrette. She placed her house key on a chain around her neck and wrote a quick note to Betty not to worry in case she woke up before Anne got back. She then slipped out the door and into the elevator. Before Anne left the lobby of the apartment building, she did a few knee bends and leg pulls to warm up, then raced outside into the light drizzle and made her way towards Central Park.

She hated running. And if there was anything she hated more than running, it was running in the rain. Yet, here she was, legs moving and face already damp, running through the city and not minding it a bit. Running built stamina and leg muscles, and she needed both of those to win that gold medal. Running also allowed Anne to think, to clear her mind while she strengthened her body. And she had plenty to think about.

The city was at peace. The park lights were still on, and they made wavy rainbows in the puddles that now punctuated the grounds. Only the bravest of runners were out this morning, and they all seemed to be in their own worlds, just like Anne. As she made her way through the trees and up and down the inclines, she felt calm and strong. The pounding of her feet was perfectly synchronized with the pounding of her heart, and she moved lightly and rapidly around the course, arms loose, wrists dangling, head held high.

Only when her movements became automatic and painless did Anne allow herself to think. "I am going to win," she had told her coach. *I am going to win that gold medal,* she had told herself again and again. She was beginning to believe it. She thought of all the things she had won up to this point in her life. She had won a varsity letter in basketball and tennis at her old high school in Maine. She had won a place on the cheerleading squad in junior high. She had won a medal for scholastic achievement in her sophomore year in high school. She had won a stuffed animal at the county fair for pitching pennies. She had won a transistor radio for selling the most magazine subscriptions in her neighborhood. And she had won a silver charm at summer camp for her performance in the gymnastics show.

She had worked hard for everything she had won. And she could remember vividly the excitement she had felt after each success. But she knew that the thrill of winning the club championship gold medal would far surpass all the previous thrills of her life put together. For that reason, she had decided that nothing would get in her way. Homework would be dealt with as quickly as possible. Invitations from new friends at school would have to be declined or postponed. Shopping trips and sightseeing excursions would wait until after Christmas. Only one thing mattered now—winning. Careful not to do too much too soon, she slowed her gait to a walk, then warmed down with some stretching exercises.

Minutes later, she was back at the apartment removing the soggy sneakers from her feet. She dried her hair, put it back into the barrette, changed into jeans and a sweatshirt, and scurried into the kitchen in search of something to fill her empty stomach. She was pouring milk over her corn flakes when the apartment suddenly came to life.

"You're up bright and early this morning," Anne's mother said, as she plugged in the coffee pot. "Got a lot of homework?"

"Mmmm," Anne replied, her mouth full.

"Where in the name of heaven have you been?" Betty asked, rubbing her eyes as she came into the kitchen. "I saw your note on the dresser and . . ."

Mindful of her father's instructions that the girls were not to leave the house by themselves at odd hours, Anne gave Betty a ferocious look to alert her that this was to be a private matter between the two of them and not a topic of family conversation. Betty sat down at the table without saying another word, but it was too late.

"Note? What note?" Mrs. Jefferson called from the kitchen. Anne's eyes pleaded silently with Betty not to spill the beans, and Betty hemmed and hawed before answering her mother's question.

"Oh, it was just some note about going on a trip for school or something. Annie wrote it so fast I could hardly read it. Nothing important." Betty shrugged, knowing her story was not very convincing, but it seemed to do the trick. Mrs. Jefferson stopped asking questions and the subject was dropped. As Betty poured herself a bowl of corn flakes, she looked at her older sister questioningly, and Anne returned her silent queries with an expression of her own, one that promised that she would explain later. It was not until Mr. and Mrs. Jefferson were buried deep within the pages of the Sunday paper that the two girls slipped off into the privacy of their room to continue the discussion.

"Annie, what is going on with you? I wake up and start getting out of bed, and I step on a pile of wet rags. Then I find this note telling me that you went for a run and would be back in an hour. Have you flipped?"

"Calm down, Betty, and I'll explain the whole thing."

"That would be real nice of you. I hope you plan to tell me why Mom and Dad can't know about this. Were you out robbing banks this morning?"

"Honestly, Sis, banks are closed on Sundays. Can't you come up with anything more imaginative than that?"

"It would seem to me that the perfect time to rob a bank is when it's closed. Besides, I wouldn't have to use my imagination at all if you would just tell me what this is all about."

"That's what I am trying to do," Anne said, becoming exasperated. "Just sit down and shut up for a few minutes, and I'll let you in on the biggest secret of my life."

"Wow," Betty said, falling on her bed, "this may have been worth waiting for."

"OK, it all started when I had my first gymnastics lesson a few weeks ago. Remember that boy sitting near us in the stands?"

"You mean old blue eyes?"

"Yeah. Well, old blue eyes has a name. It's Greg Bartos, and I think I'm falling for him."

"Wow," repeated Betty, her eyes widening.

"Anyway, there is one major snag in our friendship. Greg has a sister, an older sister named Sarah."

"Is that the girl we saw performing your first day at the club? She was pretty good. But what does she have to do with you and Greg?"

"Well, this sister of his has blocked every opportunity I've had to get to know Greg. Every time he comes over to talk, Sarah manages to creep into the conversation or into the group. Either she's standing right there, butting in, or else Greg is telling me about how great she is and how many competitions she's won. So I finally decided that the only way to really get Greg's attention is to show him that I'm as good—if not better—than Sarah."

"How are you going to do that?"

"Well, everything seemed to fall into place

yesterday when Mr. Tompkins came over with a sign-up sheet for this annual competition held at the club. It seemed like a perfect opportunity. So, I signed up for the competition and—"

"Whoa, hold on a second," Betty said. "Let me get this straight. You're entering a gymnastics competition to prove to Greg that you're better than his sister? Isn't that just the slightest bit insane?"

"Betty, what are you trying to say?" Anne asked, irritated at her for interrupting again.

"Anne, from what I've seen of Sarah, I'd say that trying to beat her in gymnastics is like trying to outdance John Travolta. Besides, I thought you were going to the club just for fun. I thought you hated competition. The last time you entered a tournament, in camp I think it was, you told me that you felt like throwing up before, during, and after and that you would never go through that again."

"I was a child then, Betty, and unable to handle the pressure. I think I've grown up a little since that time. I can see what's really important in life now."

"You may have grown up a little since camp," Betty said, "but I doubt you've grown up that much since two weeks ago, when you were angry at Dad for even enrolling you in the club."

"Betty, don't make fun of me. Please. This is too important to me."

"Annie, I'm not trying to make fun of you. I'm just trying to understand this sudden change in attitude." Betty came over to Anne's bed and sat down next to her sister. "Anne, I haven't actually met Greg or Sarah. I don't know what they're like separately or together. But I doubt that either one of them could measure up to you in any way, and I'm sure that neither one of them is worth the fight you've got going on inside you."

Anne was grateful for her sister's words. She paused, allowing them to sink in, before continuing. "Betty, I guess this is a little harder to explain than I thought it would be. Let me try again. Greg is special. Really special. I know that I don't really know him that well yet, but every time I'm with him, even when he's talking about his sister, I just get this feeling about him. I've never felt this way before. After everything Greg has told me about Sarah, I don't know if I stand a chance in a competition against her, but I've got to try. If I beat Sarah, I can show Greg that I'm worthy of him."

"Worthy of him? Are you crazy? I think you are crazy, and I think you caught it from those two." Betty looked really angry. "It sounds to me like you've built Greg up into some kind of superhero, and somewhere in the process you've really put yourself down. You're terrific, Anne. You're special all by yourself. You don't have to compete with Sarah to be worthy of Greg. And if he can't see that, he's just not worth it. If you ask me, no boy is worth trying to make yourself into something you're not and don't want to be."

"You've never been in love before, Betty. You don't know what it's like, so don't try to give me advice." Anne was instantly sorry for her words and tried to take them back. Betty looked really hurt. "Look," Anne said, "I know this all must sound crazy to you. But it's not just for Greg that I'm doing this.

"Mr. Tompkins told me that I was a very good gymnast. He told me that last week, and I don't think he hands out compliments easily. I never mentioned it to you or Mom or Dad because I didn't want Dad to go crazy about it and sign me up for the Olympics. Yesterday the coach told me that I was every bit as good as Sarah, although I didn't have her experience. I figure that with a lot of extra work on my own I can get enough experience. I know I shouldn't let Greg be the deciding factor in how I feel about gymnastics. He *is* the main reason I signed up for the competition, I admit. But now I really want to show everyone I can do it . . . especially myself."

"OK, OK, I give in," Betty said. "I am officially offering my services. If there is anything I can do to help you out, just say the word."

Then the room was quiet. Both girls were

deep in their own thoughts until finally Betty broke the silence.

"Annie," she said, her face lighting up, "if you're really serious about getting more experience, why don't you work with the gymnastics team at school? They might not be world class, but they have all the equipment you'll need, and you'd get a chance to try some small meets before the big event rolls around."

"Betty, you're a genius," Anne said, caught up in her sister's excitement. "As soon as I have a free period tomorrow, I'll go over and talk to the coach at school and ask permission to work out with the team. This is great! What would I ever do without you?"

Suddenly Betty said, "Anne, what about Mom and Dad? When are you going to tell them about this? What's the big secret? Dad will be thrilled you're taking gymnastics so seriously. Of course, I don't know how they'll feel if you tell them you're doing it all for Greg. You'll have to come up with another explanation for your change of heart about gymnastics . . . and make it sound convincing."

"Oh, Betty, this is all too complicated. I can't explain it to them now. Will you help me keep it a secret from them for a while? Until I have a little more time to sort things out? Please? I'll do anything for you. Anything."

"Anything? How about cleaning this room for the next two weeks?"

Anne sighed and rolled her eyes melodramatically. "Oh, the sacrifices a woman must make!" And they both burst out laughing, feeling closer to each other than they had in a long time.

Chapter Six

Anne stood against the wall in the hall, talking with her friends about the biology test they had taken the previous period. Anne was relieved to find out that she wasn't the only one who was having trouble with it. Lately, she had begun worrying that she was spending too much time away from her homework, and—gymnastics or no gymnastics—her father would let her have it for that.

"Anne," Patty Morrow said, "how about if I call you up tonight and we do a little studying over the phone?" Patty was Anne's closest friend at school, and the only girl at school who knew about Greg.

"Too bad we can't get a party line," Rebecca Miller broke in. "I could use some help, too."

"In that case," Anne said, "why don't we just forget about the phone and meet here a little earlier tomorrow morning? We could go over our homework together and see how we all did."

"That sounds great, Anne," Patty answered. "If we all put our heads together from now until the end of the semester, we might be able to cope better with the final exam."

"OK, I'll pass the word around. The more people we have at our brainstorming sessions, the better it will be for me," Rebecca added.

"Hey," Patty said, relieved that the problems of homework were solved, at least for the moment, "are either of you going to that Thanksgiving party over at Sally's house? It's sort of an annual tradition, Annie, and it's usually a lot of fun."

"I'll be there," said Rebecca.

"I'm not sure I can make it, but I'll try," Anne said apologetically.

Patty grinned slyly at her. "Still after that 'trophy' at the club, huh?"

Anne smiled at Patty's code word for Greg, then became serious. "That's part of it, Pat. But I do have to work out for that meet in December. If I want to win the darned thing, I'd better get moving 'cause I'm running out of time."

"Well, you can't practice at night, can you? Come on. This party will be a blast."

"OK, OK. Guess I can't say no."

"Great. I'll call you when I get home and fill you in on the details. By the way, Annie, what did you get for the answer to question four?"

As the group of girls compared notes and answers, Betty came by and motioned to Anne from the fringe. Anne excused herself and took Betty off to the side.

"Hey, I'm sorry I had to bother you, but I'm on my way home, and I wanted to get the story straight one more time." Betty was scared and excited. She felt like a spy talking to her contact. She knew this was a mission too important to blow.

"Calm down," Anne said. "It isn't that complicated. When you get home, tell Mom that I'll be a little late because I'm studying here with some friends. If she wants more information than that, tell her some story about the test I just took, how it scared me into doing some extra work or something. Use your imagination."

"Oh, Annie, I hope I can pull this off."

"Betty, you'll do fine. Besides you won't be lying. This test was a toughie. Now get going before Mom gets really suspicious."

"Good luck," Betty hollered as she ran down the hall towards home.

"You too."

Anne turned around and said goodbye to her friends. She gathered up her books and headed for the school gym, which was located in the basement. It smelled damp, and ancient lighting fixtures gave the place an eerie, prison-like feeling. About a dozen students were working out as Anne walked in slowly and searched for a familiar face.

"Looking for someone?" said a friendly voice.

"I'm Anne Jefferson. I spoke to the coach earlier this week about working out with the team. I'd like to start today, if possible. Is the coach here?"

"No, sorry. But he did tell me to expect you. I'm Dan Molloy, team captain. I'd be glad to show you around and get you started."

"Thank you," Anne said shyly.

"Would you like to change first?"

"No, I have my suit on under my clothes."

"Good. Why don't you get ready over there, but first let me introduce you to the others." He let out a whistle, and the others looked up.

"I'd like you all to meet Anne Jefferson," Dan said. "She'll be working out with us from now on." A few people smiled and seemed friendly, so Anne relaxed.

"Where would you like to start?" Dan asked, turning to Anne.

"How about the balance beam?"

"Sure. Follow me." Sitting in a corner of the gym was the only balance beam in the room. "Pretty shabby, huh?" Dan had been examining the look on Anne's face. "We only have one of these because there are so few girls on the team. You won't have any problems getting your time on it, though. It isn't the most popular piece of equipment in the room."

"It'll do just fine," Anne said. "If you have something else you have to do, I'll be all right here by myself."

"Sorry, you won't get rid of me that easily. The coach's rules are that there have to be spotters present for every piece of apparatus in use. Besides, I had to use a lot of pull to get you over to this dark corner with me alone." Dan twirled the ends of an imaginary moustache as if he were a villain, then broke into a smile.

"Let's get to work." Anne giggled. "I think I'd feel a lot safer on that rickety old balance beam than I do standing on solid ground with you."

"You have broken my heart, sweet lady, but your wish is my command."

Anne climbed on the bar and began her routine. She was so deep in concentration she never noticed that an audience was forming around her, gazing at her with respect and awed by her ability. As she cartwheeled to the end of the bar and somersaulted off for her dismount, the team broke into applause. "I would have scored that a 9.8," Dan exclaimed, clapping. "You're really good!"

"I won't be good enough until you score the performance a perfect ten," Anne said, pleased with Dan's enthusiasm despite the score he had given her. "I'm still not good enough."

"Good enough for what?" Dan asked, bewildered by her reaction to his praise.

"Never mind. It's a long story. Can we get back to work now?" Anne had already climbed back onto the bar. Dan resumed his spotting position, confused and curious.

Afterwards, Dan followed her from the balance beam to the uneven parallel bars, from the vault to the floor mats. By the time she considered herself finished for the day, there were only two people left in the gym. Darkness had blackened the small slits of windows high up on the walls, and the clock showed that it was a quarter to six, fifteen minutes until dinner time at the Jefferson house.

"Gee, Dan, I had no idea it was so late. I'm sorry I made you stay so long."

"I stayed because I wanted to. You have nothing to be sorry about. You are really something to watch, you know that? You could teach the rest of us a thing or two."

"Thanks for the compliment, but I still have an awful lot to learn."

"Why do you keep putting yourself down that way? Why don't you admit that you're good, *really* good?"

"But not good enough."

"That's the second time you said that. What's going on inside your head? Does your father own a whip? Is your mother scrubbing floors to provide you with gymnastics lessons? Have the Olympics been rescheduled for next year?"

"I know you're trying to help, but I'm serious about all this. I have to be great, not just good, and I am doing it for me, not my parents or the glory of my country."

"Wow," Dan sighed, shaking his head, "you have really put yourself under some fantastic pressure. You must be going after one terrific prize!"

"You might say that." *If he only knew,* thought Anne.

"Anne, I'm not trying to make fun of you. I like you. I'd like to help you get whatever it is that you're after. I'd like to get to know you better, so I can understand the best way to help. How about going out with me Saturday night? I know we'd have a great time."

"Thanks a lot, Dan, but I'm afraid I can't. I'm in training for a competition, and I have to get my rest." She searched his eyes and was sorry for the disappointment and confusion she saw there. "Maybe after this is all over, we could keep that date. Besides, we'll be seeing a lot of each other at school from now on, right?"

"Sure, Anne," he said, perking up a little. "When is the competition you keep talking about, anyway? I'd like to come watch it."

"It's right around Christmas time. And, Dan, if I do win that competition, I'll owe a lot of it to you."

"Well, we'll see about that. Come on, I'll walk you home."

After the first few blocks, Anne realized that Dan was really easy to talk to. By the time they reached her door, she couldn't help thinking how funny it was that in that fifteen-minute walk she had learned more about Dan than she might ever know about Greg. But she also knew that she would never feel the same way about Dan as she did about Greg. *Boy, things sure have changed,* she mused as she watched Dan walk away. *I would have given my right arm to date a guy like that before I met Greg.*

Anne burst into the apartment. "Sorry I'm late," she called as she dropped her books on the hall table and hung up her coat.

"Did you manage to get your studying done?" her father asked, obviously relieved that she had arrived home safely.

"I haven't even made a dent in it yet. As a matter of fact, if you guys don't mind, I'd like to skip dinner and get right back to the books." Anne inched her way towards her room, hoping to get there before her father objected.

"If you have to work that hard, at least let me make you a sandwich to take in with you," Mrs. Jefferson suggested.

"Don't bother, Mom. I'll grab something in a little while. I promise. See you later." Anne ignored her sister's questioning gaze and rushed into her room. She closed the door, laid her books out on her desk, and sat down in her chair, ready to begin the studying she was supposed to have been doing for the last three hours. She tried to concentrate, but it was impossible. Images kept flashing before her eyes. First there was Sarah, challenging her, laughing at her. Then there was Greg, golden and handsome, gazing at her in admiration. Then Anne blinked and an image of Dan appeared in her mind. Was he really that handsome? Why hadn't she noticed it when she was with him? He didn't look anything like Greg, but in his own way he was just as attractive and certainly a lot easier to talk to and be with. But he just didn't make her feel the way Greg did. She couldn't explain it, and she was glad she didn't have to.

Suddenly she realized her mother was standing in the doorway staring at her. "I brought you this sandwich, dear. If you want anything else, let me know. I'll be in the kitchen." She laid the tray down and started to leave the room. But then she stopped at the door and turned back to face her daughter. "Annie, are you all right?"

"Sure, Mom, why?"

"Oh, I don't know. You seem a little different, that's all."

A little different, her mother had said. That was the understatement of the year. In a few short weeks she had forgotten all about her old life, met the boy of her dreams, dedicated herself to gymnastics, and turned down a date with a real hunk. A little different!

"No, Mom, I'm the same old Annie," she said with a smile. She was not the same old Annie, and she was glad she was not. She was happy and excited and nervous and ready for all the great things she was sure were about to happen to her.

Her mother raised a skeptical eyebrow. "Annie, what's really going on? You've been acting so mysterious lately. And your father and I aren't used to you keeping things from us. Is anything wrong?"

"Absolutely nothing is wrong, Mom. In fact, everything is very, very right."

"What do you mean?"

"Well, for starters, I'm practicing really hard for a big gymnastics meet at the club, and I'm really excited about it."

"Anne, your father will be thrilled. When did you change your mind about competing?"

"Well, Mr. Tompkins finally convinced me I was really good and should give competition a try. Besides, I want to prove something to someone."

"Who?"

"Well, there's a guy named Greg Bartos I met at the club. His sister Sarah goes there too, and Greg's really proud of her. I'm really crazy about Greg, and I think he likes me too. And I want to show him that I can be as good as Sarah."

"Anne, is that the real reason you're entering this competition? Because if it is, I think you're making a big mistake. You've got to decide for yourself what's important, not let some boy decide for you."

"You're not going to try to stop me from competing, are you, Mom?"

"Of course not. That's a decision you have to make for yourself. Besides, I'm excited for you. I think you'll do well. But it should be something you do for yourself, Anne, not to please anyone else. That's why your father and I didn't try to push you into competition in the first place. Try to remember that, OK?"

"All right. I'll try to remember."

"Good luck. I'll go tell your father the news now." She closed the door softly behind her.

Anne didn't feel like daydreaming anymore. Her mother had brought her crashing down to earth for the moment, so she opened her books and got to work at last. Why did life have to be so complicated?

Chapter Seven

"Oh, for crying out loud, Anne. Did you leave your brains home this morning? Get yourself up off that floor and back on the bars this minute, and this time see if you can manage to stay up there a little longer." The coach's face was red, and Anne knew that she had better shape up before he shipped her out for the day. She was working on an easy move, one she had done a thousand times before on the uneven parallel bars, but she just couldn't get it right this morning. She kept trying to swing from the upper bar down to the lower one, rotate around, and get back up to the upper bar for her handstand there. This was going to be her fifth try. If she botched it again, it would probably be her last for the day.

What was she doing wrong? It should have been automatic by now. She knew that the tension she felt was not helping her at all. She also knew that Greg and Sarah were sitting directly in front of her and watching her every mistake, only adding to her trouble. Why, now that it was so important to her, couldn't she get it right? She powdered her hands, looked into the exasperated face of her coach, jumped up to the top bar, and started the move again. As she built up the necessary speed and rotation, she told herself to block out everything and everyone around her and concentrate on this move completely. Her legs hit the lower bar and she folded her body around it. She got just the right snap, whipped back to the higher bar, pushed her body around backwards, and thrust herself into the handstand.

"Don't stop. You've got it. Keep going through the next turn."

Anne heard the words of her coach and loosened her body enough so that it swung down again, below and through the lower bar, up around it, and . . . rats!

"OK, Miss Jefferson. Off the floor."

Anne saw the coach approaching and braced herself for the screaming she was sure would follow. She grabbed her towel off the bench and wrapped it around her head. Maybe it would muffle a few of the coming blasts.

"What's wrong with you today?" Mr. Tompkins's tone was a lot more understanding than Anne had expected.

"I can't figure it out myself. I was trying as hard as I could."

"Maybe you were trying a little too hard, Anne. Come sit down with me for a minute." Anne followed the coach to his office, certain that anyone who was watching this scene would assume that Mr. Tompkins was about to give her a stern lecture.

"Anne," he said, after they had both gotten comfortable, "is this competition too much for you? Are you sure you made the right decision entering it?"

"It's something that I have to do."

"*Have* to do, or *want* to do? There's quite a difference, you know."

"I guess it's a little of both. Anyway, I don't want to back out. Maybe the pressure is getting to me a little bit today," Anne said, thinking about the special audience she had just held captive with her slip-ups, "but it's still a new idea for me and may take some getting used to. I'm sure I can do better if you're willing to give me another chance."

"Well, I think you've had enough for today. Why don't you work out on your own for a little while and then head for the showers. On a day like this, it's sometimes better to let things ride until you can start fresh again." Anne was grateful. Apparently Mr. Tompkins understood what was going on in his student's mind. He also knew better than to put Anne on the spot

73

about it. "I'll see you next week. And, Anne, if you want to come a little earlier, maybe we could get you started before the crowds are around to distract you."

"Thanks," Anne said, relieved. "I'll take your advice."

She ran out of the office and looked for a place to hide. The coach had understood, but she did not want to face anyone else and have to explain what had gone on inside his office. She was at the door, ready to leave the club unnoticed, when she heard that voice calling from across the room.

"Hey, Annie, wait up." She froze in place. Greg ran over to her and put his arm around her.

"Hi, Greg," she said shyly.

"Avoiding me again? Well, we have to put a stop to this. I thought we had plans for this afternoon. How about taking that tour I promised you?"

Anne's heart was fluttering. Greg hadn't even mentioned her poor showing. As a matter of fact, Greg had not even mentioned Sarah or gymnastics at all.

"I'd like that," she said. "Let me make a quick phone call home, and I'll be ready to go."

"Great," Greg said. "I'll shower and change and meet you back here."

Anne picked up the phone and dialed her number. She was glad that Betty was the one who answered the phone. "Betty, tell Mom that I'm not coming home right away, but I'll be back for dinner."

"Anne, do I have to lie again? It almost made me faint the last time."

"No little sister, you can tell the truth. I'm going out on my first date with Greg. Tell the whole world about it for all I care. Sing it out the window."

"Hey, Anne, that's great. I'll tell Mom right away. Have fun."

Anne cradled the phone. She was flying. Only with the utmost effort did she manage to calm down before Greg emerged from the locker room dressed and ready to go.

"I'm starved," he announced. "How about starting this tour with a little lunch at a great health-food store I know down in the Village?"

Anne hated health food and had no idea what village he was referring to, but it didn't matter. "Sounds great," she said. Greg took her hand in his and led her out the door. *Feels great, too*, she thought with a smile.

It was the brightest, sunniest day Anne could remember. The very air crackled with excitement and promises. She stared out the window of the Fifth Avenue bus and watched the city streak by. The bus was crowded. Anne and Greg had been able to find seats in the back, but conversation was impossible because of the noise. And as far as Anne was concerned, it was just as well, for she was too excited to talk, and her words probably would have come out in a jumbled mess. Sitting this close to Greg, having him all to herself, and thinking about spending an entire afternoon with him alone was all she could handle right now.

Greg tapped her on the shoulder and motioned towards the door, indicating that their stop was coming up. As Anne inched her way through the crowd, she felt a knot beginning to form in the pit of her stomach. The day she had been waiting for and dreaming about was finally here, and she was scared. Would it live up to her expectations? Would Greg be all she imagined him to be? Would she be able to find enough things to talk about to keep him from getting bored? Only after they had escaped from the bus and Greg had taken her hand again did she began to relax. She looked over at him as he skillfully guided her through pedestrian traffic. He was so calm, so self-assured, so together. Just follow his lead, she advised herself, and you can't go wrong. They stopped at a health-food store to buy a take-out lunch before heading for Washington Square Park.

"I don't know how you do it, Anne," Greg said as he sat down beside her on a park bench. "After that mess of a lesson you had today—"

"Could we change the subject? Immediately?"

"I'm sorry. I won't mention your lesson

again. Anyway, all I was going to say was that you look beautiful."

Anne was always embarrassed by compliments and never sure quite how to respond to them. "Thank you," she managed to say, feeling herself blush.

"Tell me, girl on the street," Greg said, holding an invisible microphone to her mouth, "what is the secret of your young, healthy look?"

"I owe it all to bean sprout salads and fresh-squeezed lemonade," she answered, holding up their bag of lunch from the health-food store. "A sound diet, a sound mind, and good clean living are the secrets of my success." They both cracked up.

Then Greg asked, "Are you really into health food?"

"Sorry, but the real secret of my success is hamburgers, french fries, and chocolate shakes. Oh, and an occasional pizza when I can fit it in."

"A junk-food addict! What have I gotten myself in for?"

"There's still time for you to escape," Anne said, laughing. "I'd never be able to find you in this crowd. Actually, I'd never be able to find my way home, so please don't leave me."

"Fear not, Annie. Running away from pretty girls, junk-food addicts or not, is not my style. Let's eat. Maybe before this day is over I can convert you to good nutrition."

Anne hardly tasted her food at all. She was caught up in the atmosphere of the park and the closeness she had begun to feel with Greg. The village he had taken her to turned out to be Greenwich Village, a place she had heard a lot about. And here it was for real. She enjoyed walking through the busy streets and watching all the people pass by. There were peddlers with cowboy hats, artists in front of their easels, merchants stringing beads, children jumping rope; and food and handmade jewelry and leather goods for sale on the sidewalks. Music came pouring out of small cafes, taxicabs honked as they snaked through traffic, old men sat huddled in front of chessboards—so many things were happening all at once.

Yet, somehow in the midst of all this activity, noise, commotion, and population, Anne felt as if she and Greg were the only two people in the world. It was an old cliché, Anne thought, but she didn't care. She was in love. It felt wonderful to admit it and even more wonderful to be experiencing it. She felt like shouting it to the world. Another cliché—so what? It was how she felt. It was how she wanted to feel. She looked over at Greg for the thousandth time that afternoon and wondered what he was feeling. She searched for a sign, a smile, an expression that would indicate what he was thinking, but she came up blank.

"Are you all right, Annie?" Greg asked, meeting her intense stare.

"Oh, fine," Anne said, embarrassed for getting caught.

"Have you had enough of this craziness for a while? We could move our act uptown to a quiet museum, or go window-shopping, or find you a hamburger."

"How about all three, not necessarily in that order?"

"Well, I must admit that I underestimated you. I was sure that after this morning you wouldn't have any energy left at all."

Anne was really hurt. "I thought you weren't going to mention that again," she said.

"Calm down, Anne. I was only kidding. Come on, let's catch the bus." Then he smiled and Anne smiled back.

The rest of the afternoon sped by. Greg took her to the Whitney Museum, and Anne discovered treasures far different from those housed in the Met: works that were very imaginative, more modern, and more difficult to understand. Then they went to F.A.O. Schwarz, the famous toy store. Further down Fifth Avenue they stopped to admire the diamonds in the window of Tiffany's and the fashions in the windows of Saks. They bought hot dogs from a curbside vendor and ice cream from a bicycle freezer, and they held hands and talked and talked and talked.

"Boy, this city is incredible," Anne gasped as the afternoon drew to a close. "Where else could you get a sixty-cent hot dog and a five-thousand-dollar dress on the same block?"

Greg laughed. "I guess it is pretty amazing when you put it that way. Still, it all comes down to money."

"That's a pretty grim thing to say."

"Well, you can't help thinking about it once in a while. I'll be going to college soon, then medical school, then—"

"Whoa! You never told me you wanted to become a doctor. When did you decide that?"

"I've wanted to become a doctor for as long as I can remember. I guess I never talk about it much because I'm not sure I'll make it that far. That's a lot of school, and school costs a lot of money. I don't know if my parents can swing it with all the extras they're paying for already."

"Well, if you want it badly enough, you'll find a way. There are lots of scholarships and there must be plenty of state schools in New York that are less expensive than most."

"I've thought about all that. I've been working my tail off in school to be able to get one of those scholarships. I've sort of convinced myself that that's the way to go. You see, I dream about going to Harvard Medical School. I'm not a snob or anything, but if you're dreaming, why not dream about the best?"

"Greg, you'll make it. I know it. Dreams can

come true." Anne fell silent. She wasn't thinking about Greg's dreams any longer, only her
own.

"Do you know what you want out of life,
Annie?" Greg asked, reading her expression.

"Not really. Nothing specific yet, that is."

"Well, I really want to be a doctor. I want to
contribute something. I want to be able to look
back someday and be proud of myself—what I
did, what I became, how I got there, and who I
helped along the way. Does that make any
sense?"

"Sure it does," Anne said just above a whisper. "I think that's terrific."

"Wow, it's getting late," Greg said suddenly, looking at his watch. "I'd better get you home
before your parents call out the vice squad."

As they hurried home along the busy sidewalks, Anne asked, "How is *your* training for
the competition going, Greg? Do you mind if I
come watch you on the big day?"

"Of course I don't mind, but I don't have a
chance of winning it this year. There are three
or four guys who are training for the Olympics
at the club, and I don't come close to their
talents. I'm just in it for fun, anyway. I'm sure
you know what I mean."

"No, I don't. Not exactly." Was he implying
that she didn't have a chance either?

"Come on, Annie, be realistic. I know I'm
good, but not that good. And I've seen you work

out. You're good, too, but you have to know that Sarah is going to run away with the title. She's done it for the last four years, and there's no reason why she won't be able to do it again."

I can think of at least one reason, Anne reflected. "I'm not so sure," was all she said.

Greg continued, not even hearing what Anne had said. "I'll be really proud of her, of course. I always am. And you know, even with the strain of her own competition facing her the next day, she always comes to watch me the day before. She knows how much it means to have a friendly face in the crowd, someone cheering you on."

Anne was hurt. Hadn't he heard her say that she, too, would be there to watch him? Wasn't her face friendly enough or her cheering loud enough to make him happy? Why did he have to bring up Sarah again? Did he really feel that Anne didn't have a chance of beating his sister?

Now she had two problems to overcome, Anne realized as they turned the corner of her block. First, she had to beat that girl and do it convincingly. It couldn't look as if the judges got tired of the same old winner and gave the underdog a break in the scoring. She would have to be so perfect that there wouldn't be any doubt.

Then, she had to find something really gorgeous to wear to the ball after the competition. Of course, it really wouldn't matter that much what she wore, with the gold medal wrapped around her neck. On second thought, maybe she wouldn't need to get a dress at all. She hadn't even been invited to the ball yet! Greg would probably escort Sarah, and Anne had no intention of showing up with her father as escort.

Anne was so rapt in thought, she didn't realize that Greg had been talking to her. Now they were standing in front of her apartment, and Greg was saying goodbye.

"I'm sorry, Greg. What did you say?"

"I said that I had a great time, a wonderful day, and that we should do it again next week after practice. Can you make it?"

"I think so," Anne said, knowing full well that she would be there.

"I promise I'll find you a hamburger, french fries, and a chocolate shake if you'll say yes now."

"Then it's a deal."

As Anne grabbed the knob and started to open the door, Ggeg took her hand one last time and pulled her over to him. He put his arms around her waist, looked deep into her eyes, then kissed her softly on the lips. Anne's eyes were closed, and she felt weak. She was sure that if Greg let go of her too suddenly she would faint right there.

"I'll see you next week," he whispered. "I can't wait."

She watched him walk down the hall, get on the elevator, and disappear. She was still in a state of shock, and as she leaned on her door, it slipped open and she fell crashing to the floor.

"That's quite an entrance," her mother exclaimed, rushing over to her side. "Are you all right?"

"Don't worry, Mom," Anne reassured her mother. "I'm just fine."

"Well, your bottom may be on the floor, but your head seems to be somewhere in outer space," Mrs. Jefferson said, smiling. "How about filling me in on all the glorious details?"

"Nothing would make me happier than to relive this day," Anne said, pushing herself up off the cold tiles. "Come on in my room. I could use a soft bed to sit on right about now." Anne laughed as she pirouetted down the hallway to her room. When she and her mother had gotten comfortable, Anne told her story in vivid detail, leaving out, of course, the part about Sarah and the very private kiss at the door. After her mother left, Betty burst into the room.

"Oops. Sorry, Annie. I'll leave you alone in just a second. I have to get a book."

"No, Betty, sit down. You're just the person I wanted to see."

"Really? OK, so how did it go today?"

"Except for one little speech about his perfect sister, the day was wonderful. Betty, he kissed me goodbye, and he made another date for next Saturday before he left. Can you believe it?"

"Yup, I believe it. I've been telling you all along that you were good enough for him. Now maybe you'll realize that you don't have to knock yourself out to win a stupid tournament to get Greg."

"No, Betty, you're as wrong as you can be. I have to win it now more than ever."

"But why?" Betty was totally confused. "He likes you. You don't have to prove anything to him."

"But Sarah is still going to keep coming between us. The only way to put her out of the picture is to put myself in the spotlight."

"Anne, have you ever thought about the possibility that if you do win this competition and put Sarah to shame, you might just shatter Greg's image of his sister without winning anything for yourself?"

Anne had to think for a long time before answering that one. Betty might have a point. But on the other hand, Betty didn't know Greg the way Anne did. Finally she said, "Greg really admires winners, Betty. I just know he'll be incredibly proud of me if I win that competition—even if I have to defeat his sister to do it."

"Anne, if you really think you're doing the right thing, I already told you that I'll help you any way I can. Just remember that winning isn't everything."

"It is to Greg."

"OK, I give up, I tried. Dinner's ready. Are you coming?"

"I'll be right in." Betty had made sense in a way, but Anne was sure her own logic was right. She had spent the day with Greg, she had gotten to know him, she had discovered that he cared about her. It was all true. She wasn't just dreaming anymore. It had become real, and her need to win that medal had become more important than ever. There was no turning back now.

Chapter Eight

It was the end of November. Thanksgiving had come and gone. The days were colder and darker and seemed to go by faster. The city already sparkled with Christmas lights and the shop windows were filled with elves and reindeer. Chestnuts roasted on open fires, and skaters whirled around the ice in Rockefeller Center. Mrs. Jefferson took out the carton filled with thermal underwear, boots, hats, and gloves. The lights stayed on longer, and the thermostat in the apartment was turned up.

But Anne couldn't have felt any warmer or happier. She was in love, and that made all the difference in the world. Nothing in her life had ever come close to the excitement, anticipation, and optimism she felt now. Since that first date, she had spent every Saturday afternoon with Greg. They had walked through the zoo, ridden on the Staten Island Ferry, toured the United

Nations, gone to the top of the Empire State Building, seen a play, skated in the park . . . and fallen more and more in love. Although neither of them had ever said the words, Anne was sure of her devotion to Greg and was pretty sure he felt the same. Oh, it was great to be alive and to be in love. The whole world seemed friendlier. Every day brought new experiences. Life became more fun.

Anne's time at the club had taken on a more relaxed glow, too. Things were coming easier to her now, and her confidence in her ability to win the gold was growing daily. Everything she tried—backrolls and splits on the balance beam, pike somersaults over the vault, triple twists in her floor exercise, or reverse grips and fallaways from the uneven parallel bars—came easily to her now.

She had continued her routine of arriving early at the club to work uninterrupted and unobserved with Coach Tompkins, and it had paid off. Not only was she relieved of the usual strain of practicing in front of Greg, but she also felt that she was getting a much needed jump on Sarah, who had no idea how much Anne was improving.

Only last week, the coach had complimented Anne on her skills and determination. He made her feel that she was beginning to have a real chance of winning. Winning. Winning. Anne still could not get that word out of her mind. In fact, it had become so important to her that she was spending more and more time at the club and less and less time with Greg. Gymnastics became her first priority. She was devoting so much of her life to it that she had almost lost track of why.

"Anne," Mr. Tompkins had told her after her last lesson, "I'm impressed. You've come so far in so short a time that I almost can't believe it. I always knew that you had talent. I just never knew you had the determination to match it. It's going to be quite a tournament this year, and I can't wait to watch it."

"Coach," Anne had asked, "what can I do between now and December to get myself really ready?"

"I have only two suggestions. All of your lessons have been private. You ought to try working out in front of a crowd. I don't want you to fold the first time you have people watching you. Remember the women's tournament is held right before the ball, so it draws a big crowd. The people usually figure that they'll watch the women's competition and then head straight for the Plaza. They time their arrivals that way. Besides that, the finals are held under spotlights, and that puts on extra pressure. If you're not ready for it, those lights can make you feel like you're the center attraction in a three-ring circus."

89

"You said you had two suggestions. What is the other?"

"Well, you might want to work out with Sarah Bartos. If anyone can give you that little extra touch of polish you need to top things off, she can." Anne was ready to reject the idea immediately, but she listened to what the coach had to say, and it made sense. Why not work out with Sarah? That would let her look over the toughest competition. And, of course, Anne didn't have to show Sarah everything she could do. She could hold back a little so Sarah wouldn't suspect how good Anne really was.

That's exactly what Anne did. At first, she was surprised by Sarah's willingness to help out, even thrown off guard a little by how friendly she seemed. Sarah constantly offered tricks to help smooth out a move or suggested a new move to add difficulty to Anne's routine. And perhaps most important of all, the two of them working out together always drew a small crowd of spectators, giving Anne the audience exposure she needed.

Anne was sure that Greg understood her spending so much time at the club. Although he questioned her about it once or twice on their shortened dates, he never made it an issue. She was sure he realized that all this extra work and practice was for him.

Finally, the last day of practice before the competition arrived. The club was much quieter than usual as each contestant concentrated on last-minute preparations.Everyone was hard at work, and not a single piece of apparatus was left idle. The benches were empty. Only when the coach asked for everyone's attention did the frantic activity stop. The members of the club gathered around Mr. Tompkins and took seats on the practice mats in the center of the room.

"Ladies and gentlemen," Mr. Tompkins said, "I would like to take this opportunity to wish you all the best of luck next week. I have watched all of you work tremendously hard over the last few months, and I am sure this will be one of the finest competitions in the club's history. I look forward to seeing you all on Saturday and Sunday, but right now I want you to go home. Read a book. Listen to music. Take a hot bath. You're all as good as you're ever going to be by next weekend, and the best thing to do for the next few days is forget all about gymnastics and have some fun. Don't allow one serious thought to creep into your heads before you come back here for the big event. And now, get lost. I'm locking the place up. Again, good luck to all of you."

As the crowd began stirring and scurrying off in different directions, Greg went over to Anne and said, "I'll meet you by the door in ten minutes. Let's have lunch. I want to talk to you."

"OK," Anne said. This sounded serious. What did Greg want to talk about? Did it have to do with the competition? Did it have to do with their relationship? She changed into her clothes as fast as she could and headed for the door, where Greg was waiting.

"Ready?" he asked with a smile.

He was smiling. That was a good sign.

"Ready," she said, hopefully.

As they emerged from the warmth of the gymnastics club, the icy cold of December in Manhattan slapped them both in the face. Anne wrapped her heavy coat around herself protectively, and slipped her gloves over her already stiff fingers. She began to tremble, but she wasn't sure if it was from the cold or from her anxiety over what Greg had to say to her. As she took his outstretched hand and walked beside him, she couldn't shake the dread she felt.

"Are you too cold to walk down Fifth Avenue, Anne? The store windows are really something to see right now."

"Are you kidding? I come from Maine, remember? This is like spring up there." They turned the corner of Fifth Avenue, and Anne was about as cold as she'd ever been. In Maine she had worn thermal underwear on days like this, but she didn't want to tell Greg that.

Anne and Greg walked slowly down Fifth Avenue, admiring all the lovely displays they passed. The more they walked, the more Anne felt as though she had left the big city and entered a fairyland. One window had a typical Christmas scene, complete with jolly Santa, hard-working elves, and reindeer. The next window had a miniature city with tiny boats sailing in the magical harbor and electric trains running around the border. It was like a dream. She was looking at Greg, wondering what she could buy him for Christmas that would be truly special, when he led her into the welcoming warmth of a coffee shop.

"Will this table do?" Greg asked, as he guided Anne into a booth at the very back of the coffee shop.

"Fine," Anne said, hearing the warning siren going off in her brain. She ordered a cup of hot chocolate and sat back, ready for anything.

"Anne," Greg said, very seriously, "there's something I've wanted to talk to you about for a long time now. I just haven't been able to decide how to do it." He paused. He was still unsure. He stared at the table, searching for the right words. "I guess the best way to do this is to come right out with it. Anne, I know this is the last minute and everything, but would you be my date for the ball?"

Anne couldn't help her reaction. She threw her head back and laughed so hard that tears flooded her eyes and ran down her cheeks.

Greg looked hurt and bewildered. "Anne,

please don't laugh at me. I know you probably have a date already. I was stupid to wait so long."

Now Anne swallowed her laughter with a painful gulp. "Oh, Greg, I'm sorry. Honestly I am. It's just that I expected you to tell me something horrible today. You sounded so serious back at the club that I got really worried. Your invitation came as such a relief that I guess I got carried away. Of course I'll go to the ball with you. I wouldn't think of going with anyone else."

Greg smiled. Then he frowned. "Anne, you're very important to me. Have I ever said or done anything to make you doubt that?"

How could she tell him how she felt about Sarah? How could she explain her feelings of not being good enough for him? "No," she lied, "I've never doubted you."

"Good," he answered, apparently relieved, "because you really are very important to me in many ways."

Why did she feel a "but" coming on? What had he left unsaid, afraid of hurting her feelings? Why was the trembling returning to her hands now? Anne mustered all her courage and asked the question that had racked her brain for so long, the scariest of all questions. "Greg, how would you feel if I beat Sarah next week? I mean, what if I win the all-around title from her this year?"

Greg stared at her as if the possibility had never entered his mind. He didn't have to say a word as far as Anne was concerned. The answer to her question was written all over his face. Anne felt as if she were staring into a neon sign, flashing a message to her over and over again. YOU WON'T WIN. YOU CAN'T WIN. YOU'LL NEVER BE AS GOOD AS SARAH. Anne turned her face away and fought back the urge to cry.

Greg leaned over the table and took her hand tenderly in his. "Annie, look at me," he whispered. Slowly, reluctantly, she raised her eyes to his. "You know I would be very happy for you if you won. I'd be really proud. After all, that would mean I would get to escort the winner to her victory ball."

Again Anne sensed a hidden "but" wandering around in his thoughts. All right. She wasn't stupid. She could fill in the blanks for herself. *I would be happy for you. I would be really proud . . . BUT I don't think you have a chance.* That's what he meant. Now it was all out in the open. Now she knew for sure that she had to win that competition. Without that victory Greg would continue to compare Anne to Sarah, and Anne would always come out losing. *OK, Mr. Bartos, I've got your number. You'll get to escort the winner to the ball, no matter how much you doubt it now. I'll win that competition and I'll win you.*

"I'm glad to hear that, Greg," she said at

95

last. She spoke softly, trying to hide the determination building inside her. "I'm really looking forward to it, too."

Then he was smiling at her again, and she forgot about everything else. He looked around behind him to make sure they were not being watched. Then he leaned over the table and kissed her. When their lips parted, he got up from his seat and walked around to her side of the booth. There, sheltered from the eyes of other customers, he kissed her again, holding her close to him the whole time.

As he moved his lips from her mouth to her eyes, he stroked her hair and breathed softly in her ear.

Wherever he touched her, she felt sparks flying. Her skin burst into goose bumps. Her mind went blank. She felt as if her body had been emptied and then filled with soft, fluffy clouds. She was no longer sitting. She was floating.

"Are you ready for your check?" The waitress hovered over them, obviously amused by what she had seen. Greg straightened up, embarrassed and annoyed at the intrusion. He glared at the waitress.

"Excuse me," she said, "are you ready for the check?"

"Yes," he said through gritted teeth. He grabbed the check from her outstretched hand, scanned it briefly, and withdrew the money from his pocket. As the waitress disappeared, Greg helped Anne on with her coat and led her out the door. It didn't seem as cold out there anymore, even though the sun had set an hour ago. "Come on. I'll walk you home."

"Greg, would you mind if I went home by myself this time? It's only five blocks from here, and I sort of want to clear my head before I have to face the family."

Greg seemed pleased that he had had such an effect on her. "OK, I'll call you later."

Anne kissed him on the cheek and started off. As soon as she was out of his view, she began running. She ran through the crowds, she ran across streets, and she didn't stop running until she had run up to her front door. "Betty!" she yelled. "Betty!"

"He asked you? Did he, Sis? Did he ask you to the ball?"

"Yeeeeessssss!"

"Hooray!" Betty roared, practically lifting her sister off her feet and spinning her around.

"For heaven's sake, what's all this screaming about? Has the city been invaded?" Mrs. Jefferson asked, laughing.

"Mom, Greg asked me to the ball after the competition next week. He really did."

"Well," Mrs. Jefferson smiled, "that's wonderful dear."

"Wonderful? That's hardly the way I would describe it. In fact, I can't think of a single word that could describe how I feel. It's like I became Cinderella overnight."

"Well, Cinderella, I don't happen to have my magic wand with me, so it seems to me that we have some shopping to do. You're on vacation next week. Why don't we start looking for that perfect dress on Monday?"

"Oh, Mom, all the stores are open late tonight because of Christmas. Couldn't we go now, after dinner?"

"Well, your father was called to the office a few minutes ago and won't be home for quite a while. All right. You eat your dinner, then find me a pumpkin, change it into a taxicab, and we'll head downtown."

"Mom, you're the greatest," Anne said as she rushed to the dining room table and started wolfing down her food. Betty agreed to stay home and do the dishes, so it was only half an hour after her grand arrival home that Anne made her departure along with her fairy god-mother.

Even though the stores were jammed, sales clerks were impossible to find, and lines wrapped themselves around the cashiers like hungry snakes, Anne had a wonderful time. She and her mother had developed a system over the years whenever they went shopping in Boston. First they would select several dresses for Anne to try on. Then Anne would go to the dressing room while her mother stayed on the floor looking more thoroughly through the racks, selecting additional possibilities and bringing them in to Anne. This kept the flow continuous and eliminated the nuisance of having to get dressed each time to look for new choices.

The system had always worked well, but this time Anne was faced with a problem she had never had before: just about every dress she tried on seemed perfect, and she couldn't decide which one she wanted—until her mother reappeared at the dressing room curtain. "Are you ready for this one yet?" she asked slyly.

"Sure," Anne said, "one more won't hurt." Her mother slid the gown through the curtain, and Anne saw its reflection in the mirror in front of her. Her eyes widened, and she let out a gasp. "That's it!" she exclaimed. "That's the one."

"Come on, try it on. I'm dying to see how you look in it." Anne's mother hopped into action. She carefully took the dress off the plastic hanger and slipped it over Anne's head. She zipped and hooked and adjusted, and then she moved back to take it all in. "That's the one, all right. Cinderella herself would be envious."

Anne stared at herself in the full-length mirror. There was nothing she could say. The maroon satin gown clung to her body as if it had been made for her. The low-cut neckline showed off her new curves, the short bell sleeves hid the muscles in her arms about which she had always been self-conscious, and the full ballooning skirt was perfect for dancing. The glow of the maroon satin highlighted the color in her cheeks and brought out the hints of red in her golden brown hair. The dress was perfect.

"It's beautiful," Anne said.

"*You're* beautiful," Mrs. Jefferson said. "I had no idea how much you had grown up. Isn't it silly that it took a dress to make me realize that my little girl has become a woman?" Tears filled her eyes.

"Come on, Mom. Don't get mushy on me now, or I'll start crying too. Let's get this dress safely home before we get it all wet."

"Not so fast. There are still a few stops we have to make."

Mrs. Jefferson led Anne to the shoe department. They purchased a pair of gold shoes, high-heeled and open-toed. In the jewelry department they bought a pair of earrings and a necklace to match. Finally, Mrs. Jefferson bought a pair of elegant combs, studded with golden sequins for Anne's hair. Her outfit was complete. The shopping bags were full.

When they arrived home, Betty met them at the door. "Just in time, Anne, there's a phone call for you. It's a guy and he sounds cute. I was about to take a message when I heard you come in. You also have a thousand phone messages from your friends. They're on your desk."

"Is it Greg?" Anne asked.

"No, he said his name was Dan."

"Thanks, Betty. I'll take it in our room. Hang it up out here for me, will you?" Anne dumped her packages on the hall floor and rushed into the privacy of her room. She sat at her desk and picked up the phone.

"Hello, Dan."

"Hi, Anne. I hope I'm not calling you at a bad time."

"No, not really. I just got back from a shopping trip with my mother."

"Christmas presents?"

"Nothing that exciting," she lied.

"Well, I just wanted to call and say hello. Now that school's closed for vacation, I haven't seen you for a while, and I was wondering how you've been. What have you been doing with yourself now that I'm not around to entertain you daily?"

"Oh, I've been keeping pretty busy. That tournament I told you about is next week, and I've been trying to put the finishing touches on my routines to get ready for it. Besides that, I've just been hanging out. You know what I mean."

"Boy, does that sound boring. It seems to me that all you ever think about anymore is gymnastics. Why don't I take you out one day this week and show you that there's more to life than the balance beam?"

Anne hesitated. Dan's words hit home, and

she started to worry. Was gymnastics all she thought about anymore? Was she becoming boring? How could she tell Dan that there was something else on her mind—someone else—without hurting his feelings? "Dan," she stammered, "I—I don't think this week is a good time for me. I'm really exhausted from all the training and everything. You understand, don't you?"

"I think I'm beginning to. Anne, if you don't want to go out with me, why don't you just come out and say so? I'm a big boy. I can take it."

Good question, Dan, Anne thought. *Why am I so reluctant to tell him about Greg? Maybe it's because I'm not sure enough of Greg myself. Still, it isn't fair to string Dan along because of my own insecurities.* "Dan," she said slowly, "I guess you have a right to know that I'm sort of involved with someone else right now. I like you a lot, but I'm just not the kind of person who can handle two guys at the same time."

"Well, why didn't you say so? Anne, we know each other well enough to be honest with each other. Is this guy someone from school?"

"No, he's a friend of mine from the gymnastics club." Anne felt uncomfortable about the way the conversation was going. Still, she was relieved that Dan was taking her rejection so well, and she felt she owed him an explanation.

"Aha!"

"What does that mean?"

"Just aha. Now I know why you've become so devoted to your sport."

"Come on, Dan. Give me a little credit. If I were dating a skydiver, you can bet I wouldn't be spending my free time jumping out of planes. I really am training for a meet."

"OK, relax. I was only kidding. Boy, you're really touchy tonight."

"I'm sorry. It's been a long day. Dan, I want you to know that you're one of my closest friends here in New York. I hope this doesn't spoil our friendship. I didn't mean to hurt your feelings."

"You didn't. Well, maybe a little, but I'll get over it soon enough. And I'll be around. Don't you worry about that."

"Thanks for understanding. That means a lot to me."

"Well, as long as we're such good buddies, can I come and watch you in this tournament of yours? You can never have too many supporters on your side."

"Oh, Dan, that would be so great! I'm so nervous about it, and having you there would really help me a lot. The competition is on Sunday morning, nine o'clock, and it continues throughout the day. The finals are that night. Can you make it?"

"I'll have to check it out with my parents. We're having Christmas company in from out of town, but I'm sure I can get away for a while. I'll be there for some of it, Anne. I promise."

"You're the greatest," Anne said. She meant it. She hadn't known many people in her lifetime who would put themselves out for her the way Dan would. It made her feel really special.

"Well, listen, Anne, good luck on Sunday. Remember, I'll be there. Until then, rest up and relax. I'll talk to you soon."

"Bye."

Anne hung up the phone and leaned back in her chair. *What a nice guy,* she thought. *How lucky I am to have a friend like Dan.*

Chapter Nine

The Metropolitan Gymnastics Club was empty. It was seven o'clock Sunday morning on the day of the women's competition. No one else had arrived yet. It was eerie. It was peaceful. It was terrifying.

Anne walked slowly and deliberately around the polished wooden floors, turning around every time her soft steps echoed and bounced off the hollow walls. She had hardly been able to sleep a wink last night, and when she had finally given up trying at six o'clock in the morning, she decided to escape the speeches of luck and words of wisdom from her family by sneaking away before they got out of bed. She had made it to the club in record time, and now that she had arrived, she was not quite sure what to do with herself.

The club looked very different. All the apparatus, except for one balance beam, one uneven parallel bar, one vault, and one large floor mat, were gone. Most of the rows of benches had been set up in one area, decorated with red, white, and blue streamers and padded for extra comfort. An enormous sound system had been installed, and spotlights loomed threateningly in every corner. Four small desks, complete with paper, pencils, and scoring displays sat opposite the stands, dominating the whole setting. Then, of course, there was the roster of female competitors, listed alphabetically and numbered from one to sixteen. Sarah Bartos led the list, with Anne Jefferson stashed conveniently someplace in the middle. Spooky. The place was definitely spooky. She shivered from the chill creeping up her spine. All at once she felt exhausted, out of place, and scared out of her mind. The light breakfast she had somehow managed to eat was beginning to slosh around inside, and she felt sick. She rushed into the locker room and got there just in time to get rid of it.

What a fine start, she told herself. *Pull yourself together*. She changed into her leotard, covered it with a sweatsuit, rolled her hair up and secured it with pins, and went back into the arena.

Workmen had arrived and were busy testing out the lights and the sound system, moving furniture around, and polishing the apparatus. Anne retreated to her favorite corner and sat down. If she had any hope of concentrating this morning, she had to first empty out all the cobwebs of thoughts hanging from the corners of her mind. She knew they had to be swept out to make room for the upcoming, important thoughts. She rested her head against the wall and closed her eyes.

The first image she saw was of Greg. He had been wonderful in the competition yesterday. He had seemed so sure of himself, so physically and mentally in control. Yet, he hadn't won a single award. He had been right when he sized up the competition. Four other men placed above him in each event, and he had come away with the fifth-place miniature medal for one of the individual events. Not a bad showing at all, and he had seemed pleased with it. That was all that counted. They had watched the all-around finals together, huddled in the bleachers, and Anne had marveled at the way Greg had cheered on the men who had defeated him earlier. That was class. She doubted she would have been able to do the same.

The preliminaries were scheduled to begin at nine o'clock. At eight forty-five the stands were filled with families and well-wishers. The judges were poised at the desks. The club buzzed and hummed with muffled sounds of anticipation. Coach Tompkins called the sixteen competitors into his office. Sarah gave Anne a pat on the back as they followed the coach across the floor and wished her good luck. Anne became very uncomfortable. As they crowded into the glass cubicle, Mr. Tompkins took a seat behind his desk and shuffled through some papers on his clipboard. At last, he raised his eyes to the group.

"Good morning," he said. The group responded tentatively. "I see that you are all here, so there is no need to call the roll. I would just like to say a few words to all of you about how we'll be running this operation. It's not all that complicated, so if you pay attention, we can get through this in a few minutes and start the meet on time." Again the coach checked his papers. He placed his hands flat on his desk and pushed back his chair. Anne's torment mounted. She shot a glance over to Sarah, hoping to catch her in a moment of weakness. But Sarah seemed unflustered. She smiled and gave Anne the thumbs-up sign. Great.

"Now," Mr. Tompkins said at last, "since we have sixteen competitors and four events, we will be dividing you up into groups of four. You will remain in your original group throughout the competition and rotate throughout the various apparatus together. We would appreciate it if you would all stay by your group, even if it's not your turn to perform. We don't want to have to search through the crowd for you every five minutes." The coach listed the groups and where each group would start. Anne was relieved that she had not been placed with Sarah. She was also happy that she would begin the competition in her worst event, the vault, and work her way up to her best event, the balance beam. She prayed silently that all the judges were in good moods and had had a good night's rest.

"Now, as far as the finals are concerned we will be taking the top four scorers from the morning events to compete in the finals. You will start fresh in the evening. Your morning marks will be disregarded. Those of you who make it that far will have a break for lunch and time to rest. The finals will begin around five tonight. Anyone not there on time will be disqualified. Does everyone understand?" The sixteen young women nodded simultaneously. "All I can say now is, best of luck to all of you. Get out there and make me proud."

Anne and her group wandered over to the vault. The judges had already taken their places. The whispering crowd was suddenly silent. Anne searched the audience for a friendly face. She found her family and got winks and thumbs up from all of them. Dan Molloy was sitting next to Betty, and he clasped his hands together and shook them towards her. But Greg was nowhere to be found. Anne returned her stare to Betty and hunched her shoulders in a silent question. Betty frowned, understanding, then nodded over to the balance beam. Greg was there helping Sarah off with her jacket. He whispered something in her ear, then took a seat directly behind the chairs reserved for the four members of Sarah's group. Anne felt like screaming, "Remember me?" across the room, but bit her lip instead. She turned her attention back to the vault, pinned her number on her back, and sat down to wait her turn.

The morning went too slowly for Anne. The waiting around for her chance to perform only made her more and more nervous and drained her of her already dwindling energy. Still, by the time she had finished three of the four events she had the highest marks of her group and was trailing Sarah by only four-tenths of a point.

As her name was called for her turn on the balance beam, she searched for Greg one last time and found him, still with Sarah, but looking over at her. Her body surged with hope and spirit, and she danced her way effortlessly and flawlessly through her routine. As her feet landed squarely on the floor after her dismount, the crowd behind her broke into applause and she broke into a smile. She skipped over to the bench to wait for her score.

The judges took only seconds to tally their votes, and a renewed burst of applause came from the crowd as a 9.9 flashed up on the indicator. Anne was prompted to take a bow by the other members of her group. She waved happily to the audience, sat back down, grabbed her towel, and looked over at Greg. He had apparently missed the whole thing, for he was dusting Sarah's hands with chalk in anticipation of her uneven parallel bars routine.

Anne was hurt. She had just sparked an entire crowd to life and he hadn't even noticed! Why did Sarah keep getting in the way?

The crowd's attention was now focused on Sarah. She was the last member of her group to mount the parallel bars. She would have her turn in the spotlight now because she was the final competitor in the preliminaries. The audience was still as Sarah bounced to the high bar, and they gasped when she soared around it. Hundreds of eyes followed her every move, and hundreds of patient hands broke into applause when she finished. Her score flashed—a 9.9—and the morning was officially over, with Anne still trailing Sarah by four-tenths of a point.

"May I have your attention please," Mr. Tompkins's voice bellowed over the public address system. "Before you all leave to stretch your legs and fill your stomachs, I would like to announce the names of our four finalists in the all-around competition to be held this evening at five p.m., as well as the names of the individual winners of this morning." The crowd was hushed. "First of all, our finalists: with a cumulative score of nine-point-six, Sarah Bartos." The audience applauded politely. Anne fumed. Sarah had gotten top billing again. "In second place going into the finals with a score of nine-point-two, Anne Jefferson." More polite applause. The two other names were announced with the same results. "Now, for our individual winners. On the balance beam, Anne Jefferson." Anne was stunned. She hadn't even realized that she was in the running for anything. She turned around and smiled into the beaming faces of her family and friends, still filled with surprise and joy. Despite the fact that Sarah had managed to win the three other events, Anne was excited and encouraged. She rushed over to her parents as soon as the coach had finished his speech and was welcomed there with hugs and kisses and glowing pride.

"Well, I guess you got enough rest," Dan said slyly, planting a juicy kiss on her cheek.

"Annie, you were incredible!" Betty screamed. "Weren't you scared to death? I was shaking all over, and I was in the crowd! How did you do it?"

"I'm really proud of you, honey," Mr. Jefferson said, his face one big smile. "It's hard to believe, after your performance today, that I had to push you to get you to come here. I'm very happy for you, Anne. You were a real star out there."

Anne's mother was next. She had patiently waited on the outskirts of the family group, and she moved forward for her turn only after the rest of the clan had had theirs. "Everything they said goes double for me, Anne. You made it to the finals, and now you can relax and enjoy them because you've already won your gold medal." Anne's mother kissed her and backed away slowly.

Anne's eyes widened in amazement. "No, Mom, you don't understand. That little medal doesn't mean a thing. I can't relax yet. I have to win the finals. As a matter of fact, I have to go to the coach's office right this minute to draw numbers out of a hat for my turn. I'll be back in a second." Anne sped away, fleeing from the confusion she had caused, running towards the final hurdle to her goal.

By the time she closed the office door behind her, the coach was stirring small pieces of paper around in a plastic bowl. The three other women congratulated Anne, then stared into the bowl, hoping to pick the number that would help them most in the finals. Everyone wanted to go last. It was easier that way. You knew what score you had to earn to win. You didn't have to sit back and wait for the other girl to make a mistake. The judges were warmed up by then, and it was easier for them to give high marks after comparing you to the rest of the field.

Sarah picked first because of her morning victories. She came up with number two. Anne was next. Her hand shook as she plunged it into the bowl and continued shaking as she unfolded the slip of paper and read her number. Four. She was last. Not only was she last, but she didn't have to follow Sarah directly. Oh, everything was perfect. It was an omen, Anne was sure of it.

After the two other girls had picked their numbers, the coach refilled the bowl with tiny slips of paper. "These papers have the names of the four events on them. I'll pick these myself," he explained, "to determine the order of the final events." The coach picked out all four pieces of paper and laid them on his desk in order. The girls moved closer to his desk, peering at the papers as he opened them one by one. Anne was overjoyed. Her luck had held miraculously. First event, vault. Second event, floor exercise. Third event, uneven parallel bars. Final event, balance beam. She was starting out in her weaker exercises and finishing up strong. That meant that even if Sarah managed to build an early lead, she could catch up at the end.

Anne felt as light as a feather as she rejoined her family and Dan for lunch, but their faces were all lined with concern. "Cheer up, you guys," Anne smiled. "It's in the bag." Everyone tried to relax, and Anne noticed that Dan and Betty seemed to have gotten to know each other during the competition. They spent the whole lunch teasing each other and making jokes.

After lunch her parents went home to change into their formal wear for the ball. Dan said he couldn't attend the finals because of a family dinner engagement. Anne thanked him for coming at all and told him how much his cheering had meant to her.

Then Dan turned and said goodbye to Betty and asked her if it would be OK if he called her sometime. Betty was stunned, but she managed to let him know that it was definitely OK. Then he left, and only Betty remained behind to keep her sister company throughout the long, empty afternoon.

"Anne, I can't believe it! This has never happened to me before. Do you mind?"

"Of course I don't mind. I think it's terrific. He's a great guy, but we're just friends."

Then they walked back to the gym, and Anne stretched out on the floor behind the bleachers. Betty stayed close by. Neither of them spoke for a long time. The club had taken on its haunted atmosphere again, and talking seemed out of place somehow.

"Betty," Anne said at last, so softly that Betty had to strain to hear her, "how do you think I did this morning, really? Do you think I have a chance to win?"

"Gosh, Annie, this is hardly the time for doubting yourself. I think you were great. I've never seen you do better. You must have realized that yourself. The judges sure did."

"I know you're right. Still, one thing keeps gnawing at me. I did the best I ever did this morning, and Sarah still beat me. I just don't know if I have enough left in me to do any better, and I have to if I plan on winning."

"Once you get yourself revved up and walk out into those lights, you'll find what you need. I never thought I'd get to see you as good as you were today. Now I'm sure that you'll be even better tonight. You've come this far, Sis. Don't give up now."

"Betty, he never even once came over to me. Not one single time."

Betty knew who the "he" was without hearing any names. She felt a surge of pity flooding her because of the desperate tone of her older sister's words. Anne didn't have to say anything else. Betty had noticed that Greg had stayed close to Sarah throughout the preliminary competition. Betty saw that he had ignored Anne completely. Betty realized what that must have done to her sister.

"Annie, don't let that get you down. He probably realized that the two of you would be together all evening, so he felt obligated to stay with Sarah today."

"I suppose that could be," Anne reasoned, "but he still could have waved or something."

"You're right," Betty said, defeated. She was fresh out of optimistic words of wisdom for the time being. "Still, what you ought to be thinking about now is the finals, and if you can't concentrate on that, think about that dress hanging up in your closet and the thrill you're gonna feel when you wear it to the ball."

Anne perked up. She had felt so exhausted and drained that she had not been able to see that far ahead. Now her body felt bathed in a renewed sense of hope, of energy, of expectation. "Little sister," she said, coming alive, "I have to warm up."

The stands were packed with elegantly dressed people. Chiffon and satin and silk rustled upon the dingy wooden benches. Even the judges had changed from sloppy jeans into stylish tuxedos and ruffled gowns. The gym appeared spellbound, the audience mesmerized, the competitors charmed. The spotlights showered enchanted beams across the room, throwing glitter and sparkle on everything they touched. The stage was properly set. And Anne was nervous. Mr. Tompkins formally introduced the competitors for the benefit of those who had not attended the morning events. The scoreboard came to life, and the finals were under way.

At the end of the three events, Anne and Sarah were neck and neck. Anne had outscored Sarah on the floor exercise, and Sarah had beat out Anne on the vault. Their performances on the uneven parallel bars brought their scores even closer together, because Sarah slipped halfway through her performance and had to climb back up and start in the middle. Anne had gotten through the parallel bars without a hitch, but she could not overtake Sarah in the scoring because her routine was not as difficult as Sarah's to start with. The two other competitors were hardly even in the race. They were performing well but certainly not up to the early standards set by the two leaders.

Anne was exuberant. Her best event was coming up, and she was only trailing Sarah by six one-hundredths of a point. She knew Sarah would have to precede her on the beam, and she knew she could do better than Sarah. Her brain became a calculator as Sarah's score was flashed up on the board. 9.75. Not bad. Not great. Certainly beatable. Anne had received a 9.9 when she'd won the individual title that morning. All she had to do was repeat her performance and she would be the proud owner of the gold medal.

She heard her name called over the loudspeaker. She chalked her hands and walked over to the narrow wooden bar, full of confidence. She waited until the crowd quieted down, raised her hands in a signal that she was ready to begin, smiled, and gripped the beam in both her hands. She muscled her way into her first handstand, holding it strongly and unwaveringly for an extra few seconds. Slowly and perfectly she bent her hips into a pike position, glided her straightened legs through her arms, and lowered her bottom onto the bar. She sprang up and positioned her feet in the middle of the four-inch-wide piece of wood, cartwheeled, cartwheeled again, and turned. She hopped through her dance steps, glided through her balance steps, rolled on her back, and stood up for the last time.

Then she sucked in all the air around her. The light was shining directly into her eyes. Her heart pushed out against her chest. All she had to do now was her dismount. One last move, executed correctly, and the championship would be hers. She did her backbend and walk-over. Her positioning was perfect. She strutted the last few steps to the end of the bar, flung her body over into a somersault, twisted twice while still in the air, and landed on the ground, taking only a short step forward to retain her balance. Triumphantly, she arched her back and threw her arms over her head.

The crowd roared. They stamped their feet. They whistled and yelled "Bravo!" Anne walked over to her seat. She felt as if she were in a dream. She focused her eyes on the judges as she wrapped a towel around her. It seemed like an eternity before the judges made a move. Finally they flipped the interchangeable numbers into place and turned the board around towards the eager fans.

Anne was unprepared for the groans and hissing that came from the bleachers. Frightened, horrified, she turned her head to see her score. 9.8. It wasn't enough. She had lost by one one-hundredth of a point. Mr. Tompkins was up on the podium announcing that this year's winner of the all-around competition was Sarah Bartos.

There had to be a mistake. It was a bad dream. Anne forced herself up to the podium to congratulate Sarah. She mechanically shook her rival's hand. She stood motionless in another world as she listened to Mr. Tompkins congratulate her for being the winner of the silver medal. She felt as if she were standing outside herself watching another person go through the motions. Then all at once she felt sick, faint. She knew she had to get out of there. She had to escape the stares of the audience, the presence of Sarah, the nightmare that had become too real. As soon as the spotlights were dimmed, Anne sprinted towards the door, grabbed her tote bag, and ran. The last thing she saw as she ran from the Metropolitan Gymnastics Club was Greg embracing Sarah, patting her on the back, admiring her medal.

As Anne rushed into the streets, she realized that she had never felt more alone. Her heart ached, her body ached. She ran through the city crying, unaware of the happy Christmas shoppers and the beautiful decorations all around her. All she saw were her own tears, all she felt were sadness and horror. The competition was over. She had lost the medal, she had lost Greg, she had lost everything important. All she wanted was to curl up into a little ball and disappear.

Chapter Ten

The room was dark and silent and morbid. Racked with sobs and shaking with cold, Anne lay on her bed. She hadn't even bothered to remove her leotard, and now it was glued to her body, clinging to her like a horrible reminder of what had happened to her that evening. Still she wouldn't move, couldn't move, not even to undress. It was as if her body were trying to punish her by making her remember. It was the final burden she had to bear.

What had gone wrong? She still couldn't figure it out. Her balance beam routine had flashed through her mind a hundred times. Again and again she went over her performance in her mind, and she couldn't find a single mistake. Her toes had been properly pointed. Her movements had been graceful. Her routine had been difficult enough to score a lot of points. There was just no logical explanation. The competition couldn't have been fixed. The judges were strangers and knew nothing about Sarah's reputation. They had been fair, more than fair, all morning and had given out fair scores to every competitor. There was only one possible reason left. Sarah was better. It was hard to admit, but Anne didn't see any other possibility.

Maybe she had just been thinking of herself so much that she simply failed to notice how much better Sarah really was. If that was true, she had been the only one who failed to notice. The judges had noticed. The fans had noticed. And Greg had noticed. He had known it all along. For heaven's sake, even Betty had known it all along. Sure, they had all tried to lift her spirits with false hopes and confidence, but she had no one to blame for that but herself. She had been the one throughout the last three months who vowed that she could do it. She had been the one to tell them all that they were wrong in doubting her. She had been the one who forced them to agree with her and to egg her on in her quest for the gold. What was it Betty had said? Trying to beat Sarah in gymnastics was like trying to outdance Travolta? Why hadn't she listened to any of them? Why had she only believed them when they were saying what she wanted to hear? How could she have been so dense, so blind, so stupid?

Well, it was all over now. Sarah had won and Anne had lost—not only the competition but Greg as well. She felt like a fool. There was nothing she could do but cry. The tears she had been holding back flooded her eyes and were streamed into her pillow. Her agony surfaced through muffled moans. She felt herself sinking deeper and deeper into a state of uncontrollable depression.

"Anne, my God, are you all right?" Her father sounded alarmed. "The front door was wide open, and we were sure that someone had broken in! Annie, talk to me, please. Tell me what happened."

Rapid footsteps announced the arrival of Betty and Mrs. Jefferson. Anne could feel them all hovering over her, exhausted, confused, and worried. She forced herself to open her eyes and confront them. "I guess I forgot to close the door when I came in."

"For crying out loud, is that all you have to say for yourself?" Once her father's fears had been put to rest, his anger rose to the surface. It wasn't real anger, only the anger that comes with relief after being frightened to death. "You had us all scared out of our minds. You ran away from the club without a word of explanation and we find you here, huddled in the dark, and all you have to say is that you forgot to close the door?"

Mrs. Jefferson wrapped an understanding arm around her husband. "Why don't you go to the kitchen and make us all some hot chocolate? I think we could use the nourishment. I'll handle things in here." Mr. Jefferson nodded to his wife and left the room. Betty took a seat near Anne's desk, and Mrs. Jefferson sidled up to her elder daughter cautiously. The three of them sat there silently, waiting for the moment when the emotions would burst forth and shatter the quiet in the room. It didn't take long. Anne threw herself into her mother's arms and burst into uncontrollable sobs again. She felt her mother patting her hair and stroking her face, but nothing could relieve her pain.

"I feel like such a fool," she groaned when she was able to catch her breath.

"That condition is only temporary," her mother assured her. "If you'll stop to think for a minute, I think you'll be proud of what you accomplished today. In three short months you've worked your way to the top of the ladder. You've managed to climb higher and faster than any of us dreamed. You should be feeling proud of yourself, not sorry for yourself."

"Sorry to have to remind you of this, Mom, but I never quite made it to the top of the ladder, remember? Sarah is sitting above me on that high rung."

"And Sarah has been at it a lot longer than you have. She's been in many more tournaments than you have. Give yourself some credit, Anne, for what you've been able to accomplish in so

125

short a time. I happen to think it's quite remarkable."

"Me, too." Betty joined them on the bed. "Come on, Sis, cheer up. If you don't knock off the sobbing pretty soon, you'll look like a wreck by the time Greg gets here to pick you up for the ball."

"Don't worry about that, Betty, because Greg won't be coming."

"Did he say that to you? Did he cancel your date?" Now Mrs. Jefferson was becoming concerned.

"Can't either of you understand? Greg won't want to have anything to do with me anymore. I'm not a winner. I blew it, right before his eyes. Do you honestly think he'll want to be seen with me tonight?" The tears and pain returned simultaneously, and Anne covered her face with her hands. Mrs. Jefferson gave her daughter a little time to calm down. Then she peeled the hands away from the puffed red face.

"Now you listen to me, young lady, and hear what I have to say. You are being absolutely ridiculous about this. You won a gold medal in the balance beam. You won the silver medal in the all-around championships. I will not have anyone, even you, belittle those accomplishments. Do you really think so little of Greg that you don't believe he'll be proud of you? If he's not, Anne, then *he* doesn't deserve *you!*" Mrs. Jefferson bowed her head and sighed in an effort to control herself. "I suggest," she continued in a small, faltering voice, "that you get into a hot tub and warm yourself up. I'll bring your hot chocolate in there. After that, if you insist on continuing this nonsense, you should get into bed and get some rest. If you need anything, I'll be in the living room with your father."

"Mom, please don't be angry with me," Anne said, grabbing her mother's arm. "This hasn't been the best day of my life, you know. And I wasn't trying to put down Greg. I understood from the beginning what had to be done to really win him. I just couldn't pull it off. I don't blame him. I can't blame him for his ideals. I can only blame myself for not living up to them."

Mrs. Jefferson tried to be patient. She didn't want to upset Anne any more that night. "All right, Annie, all right. I'm sorry I raised my voice. Now get into that tub before you catch your death of cold."

Anne spent a good fifteen minutes in the warm, soothing water. She washed the perspiration from her body and the grease from her hair, and wrapped her old terry-cloth robe around her as the water ran out of the tub. As she stood in front of the mirror, blow-drying her hair, she took a good, long look at herself. Her body looked shrunken in the raggedy robe. Her eyes were puffy and lined with sadness. Her cheeks were red and her mouth was drawn and tense. What had happened? Where were the straight back and shining eyes and glowing complexion of the girl she used to be? Where was the spirit she once had, the maturity she thought she had mastered? Down the drain. It had all disappeared. It had slipped away from her in one day. She had lost all that, and Greg too, in a matter of eight hours. It was pathetic, pitiful. She could no longer stand the sight of herself in the mirror. She rushed back into her room, turned off the lights, and buried herself beneath the blankets of her bed. She couldn't face herself, and she couldn't expect anyone else to, either.

Chapter Eleven

Anne fell into a deep sleep, a dream world of happy thoughts and pleasant surroundings. Within this fantasy world she felt safe. Everything was as it should have been. She was on the balance beam, floating an inch above it, dancing and gliding in slow motion, never touching the ground. She was up on the podium, outlined in a golden glow, her medal hanging from her neck and glittering in the spotlight. She was sitting delicately upon a cloud, wafting through space with Greg by her side, embracing her, telling her he loved her, kissing her. Then there were bells, light tinkling bells, ringing the news of her victory throughout the land.

Anne opened her eyes and stared at the fluorescent dial of her clock. Eight-thirty. She let her lids fall once again, hoping to recapture the sense of peace and joy she had been experiencing. It was working. There was that bell again and Greg's voice whispering somewhere close by. It seemed so real, so near. Then it stopped. The only sound Anne heard was an awful banging coming from right outside her door. She realized that she was no longer dreaming. She was completely awake, and the noise that had roused her was a knocking on her bedroom door. She wiped her eyes, trying to bring herself out of her stupor.

"Anne, are you decent? Can I come in?" It was Greg's voice. Was she still dreaming? "Anne? Are you awake?" The door cracked open and a small beam of light flowed in from the hall. She sat up in bed, startled and confused. She reached over to her nightstand and fumbled for the light switch. As her room brightened, she stared and squinted at the figure approaching her.

"Anne, what the heck is going on?"

"Greg? What are you doing here?"

"As I recall, we had a date for this evening. I know you look lovely in anything you wear, but I really had expected something a little more formal than that old bathrobe." Now Anne was embarrassed, and she self-consciously pulled the covers up around herself. "The blankets don't help the outfit all that much. You'd better get a move on or we'll be late."

Greg started to leave the room so Anne could get dressed, when he noticed the moisture glazing her eyes. "Anne Jefferson, you tell me right this minute what is going on. Your parents seemed surprised to see me when I arrived, and now you're acting like you don't know who I am. What's wrong, Annie?"

"Greg, I don't want your pity. You don't have to take me to the dance tonight."

"I know I don't have to. I want to. I told you that last week. And why would I pity you?"

"A long time ago you told me you respected a winner. You talked about how proud you were of Sarah. Ever since I met you, I've tried to become what you wanted, to be like Sarah. In fact, I've tried to become better than Sarah because I knew that was what you wanted. Last week, when you asked me to be your date for the ball, you said you'd be proud to be escorting the winner to the ball. I'm not a winner. I'll never be as good as Sarah. I just don't have whatever it takes to be a winner."

Greg took Anne in his arms and wiped her tears away. "Look at me, Anne," he ordered. She gazed at his blue eyes and found comfort in them. "You're talking nonsense. I do respect winners, that's for sure. And I can't deny that I love my sister. Why should I deny that? I also admire her because she has a lot of fine qualities that I respect."

"Qualities that I'll never have," Anne interrupted.

"Anne, you have plenty of fine qualities of your own. Many of your qualities match Sar-

131

ah's. But there's no reason why you should want to *be* Sarah."

"Greg, every time we're together, every time we go out on a date, the conversation creeps around to Sarah at least once. Not a day has gone by without you mentioning Sarah in some context or another. I wanted you to talk about me the way you do about her. I wanted you to be proud of me and brag about me the way you do about her. Can't you see? I was sure that the only way to make you really notice me, really appreciate me, was to be like Sarah, a winner. That's why I signed up for the competition, even though I didn't really want to compete at first. That's why I worked so hard with Mr. Tompkins, even though I told him I joined the club for fun. I convinced myself that if I won that gold medal and beat Sarah, I'd be really yours." Anne broke down. She had already said too much.

"Annie, I'm so sorry," Greg said, and he tightened his grip around her. "I had no idea you felt this way. I never meant to make you feel that you you had to change for me. In my eyes you were always a winner. After your performance this evening no one in his right mind could argue with that."

"But I lost."

"No, you came in second. That's very different. And if you promise not to mention a word about this to my older sister, who shall remain nameless, I thought you had her beat all the way. You were incredible on that beam."

"How do you know? I looked over at you a few times, and you weren't even watching."

"So, I had you convinced? Good. I only hope Sarah thought the same thing. Come here, Annie. Look closely. See that little corner of my eye? Well, it was glued to you the entire evening. I was watching you all the way through the finals. I saw your performance on the beam. After that, there's no way you can convince me that you're not a winner. Besides, you've always been a winner. You don't need a gold medal to prove it to me. I can see it when you walk down the street. I can feel it when you kiss me. I can hear it in your voice. You don't have to prove anything to anyone. But if you still feel that you need tangible evidence or some sort of symbolic proof, I think I'd better give you your Christmas present a little early." Greg pulled a small velvet box from his pocket and gave it to Anne. She opened it. Cradled deep in the folds of the blue material was a small golden ring with a porcelain heart. "You won me a long time ago, Annie," Greg said softly. "I'm not sure if it was the time you got all excited about the play you'd just seen or the afternoon you gagged down that bean sprout salad or the first evening I kissed you goodbye at your door. It doesn't matter much. What matters is that I'm crazy about you and have been for a long time."

"Huh?"

"Anne, I love you. I love you for all the things you were when I met you and all the things you've become since. And if it's possible, I love you even more now than I did an hour ago because of all the things you've gone through for me. I guess I should have told you how I felt a long time ago. It would have saved you a lot of trouble. But I'm telling you now: I love you, Anne Jefferson."

"Oh, Greg, I love you, too." As they embraced and their lips met, Anne felt alive again. Somehow she had floated back up to her fantasy cloud and felt lighter than air. It was true. She could see it in his eyes. He really did love her as much as she loved him.

"Now, champ, if you don't get a move on, you're going to make us late for the ball. I'll be waiting in the living room, no matter how uncomfortable I'll feel staring at your parents for that long."

Anne giggled. "I'll rescue you from them as soon as possible. Now beat it, buster."

"Bye," Greg said, as he blew her a kiss and closed the door behind him.

Anne floated over to her closet and carefully, almost reverently, removed the hanging bag containing her gown. As she unzipped the bag, she decided that the gleaming satin dress was still a victory gown, perhaps not in the way she had originally intended, but certainly in a way she had not expected a few hours ago. She removed her old bathrobe and dabbed perfume on her wrists. She applied just a touch of makeup to her already glowing face, put on her earrings and necklace, slipped the gown over her head, and twisted her hair into wavy silk beneath her jewelled combs. Then she slipped her golden shoes onto her feet and stood back to examine herself. She was impressed. She was her old self again. Or was it her new self? It didn't matter. She looked good and she felt good. She liked herself again, and she knew that Greg loved her. What else was there that mattered? Still, Anne couldn't help feeling that something was missing, something was forgotten. As she turned around to search the room in hopes of finding a clue, her eyes came to rest on the small blue box still sitting in the middle of the bed. She rushed over to it, flung it open, and placed the tiny ring upon her finger. *There,* she thought, as she admired her gift, *now I'm ready.*

Anne should have been used to being the center of attention after the the long hours she had put in under the spotlights earlier that evening. Nothing compared, however, to the close scrutiny she was under right now in the living room of her own home. Four pairs of eyes examined her from top to bottom. Four mouths were speechless. Four hearts were filled with love. Her father just stood there with his mouth hanging open. Her mother was smiling, and Betty was jumping up and down, squealing with glee. Greg stood still as his eyes scanned her from the top of her head to her gold shoes. He didn't have to say a word. His eyes told her everything. He extended his arm.

"Let's go," he said softly.

"I'm right behind you," Anne answered.

"No, I want you by my side all evening long."

Anne was never happier. As the cries of "Have a good time" and "See you later" echoed through the hallway, Anne and Greg departed. Her dream was coming true.

Chapter Twelve

The taxi maneuvered down Fifth Avenue. On Anne's right was the quiet darkness of Central Park. On her left were some of the most expensive and elegant apartment buildings in the world. She took in a deep breath and let it out slowly. It was becoming very difficult for her to keep her excitement bottled up. She wanted to jump up and sing. She wanted to grab Greg and tell him what she was feeling, how happy he had made her. She squeezed his hand instead.

Tiny, delicate flakes of snow had begun to fall, and when Anne looked up into a street lamp, it seemed as if a shower of stars were cascading from the light onto the streets. "I guess we'll have a white Christmas after all," Greg said, staring out the window. It was the first time he had spoken since they had left Anne's apartment. Nothing was bothering him,

Anne was sure of that. She had been quiet too, caught up in her own thoughts and emotions. However, now that Greg had broken the silence she felt obliged to answer.

"I've been so involved with the competition that I forgot it was almost Christmas." What a ridiculous thing to say, Anne thought after the words had escaped from her lips. Still, it was conversation, no matter how pitiful and mundane, and she could not take it back. Oh well, he'd understand.

The cab had stopped for a red light. Greg turned to her. "Do you have any plans for Christmas Day?" he asked shyly. "I'd like you to meet my parents."

"I'd love to," Anne said, already becoming nervous at the prospect of facing Mr. Bartos. "I'm sure I could get away for a few hours after our family celebration is over. Why don't you come to my house first, visit for a while, then take me to yours. You know, my parents would like to get to know you better. They've been curious about you from the beginning."

"I can't say I blame them. I have been sort of a phantom where they are concerned. OK, you've got yourself a deal. Maybe we could go over to Rockefeller Center after all the formalities have taken place and do a little skating."

"Perfect." Then they were silent again. Anne could not tell what Greg was thinking, but she was enjoying the idea that Greg was already making plans for their future. As she looked up, her pulse quickened. There, directly ahead, was the Plaza Hotel. She had seen it during the day many times before, but at night it stood sparkling like the largest jewel in a queen's crown, a huge diamond throwing lights in every direction.

"Impressive, huh?" Greg said as the cab pulled up in front of the building. He paid the driver and escorted Anne inside. They sought a sign for the right room, found it, and made their way up a massive, winding staircase. As they reached the top of the stairs, Anne paused to take in the spectacular scene. A hundred people, at least, dressed in a hundred colors, at least, milled around before her, eating, drinking, dancing, chatting. An enormous table stretched down one entire side of the room. In the center of the table was a huge bowl of punch, and in the center of the punch was a piece of ice that had been sculpted into the shape of a swan. The ruby red fluid was flanked on either side with silver platters suspended above small blue flames. Further down the table were platters of cold hors d'oeuvres and canapés, followed by bone china plates, sterling forks, and crystal goblets. Every so often, a stiff, polite waiter picked up one of those plates and passed it through the crowd. Waitresses carried trays of champagne to the people seated at the tables scattered around the room. And all the while, the orchestra played lovely music to dance to.

"This is right out of a fairy tale," Anne whispered, afraid of breaking the spell. "I've never seen anything like it before in my life."

"Well, you'll be able to see it a lot better if you let me take you in," Greg said, smiling. "Remember, this is all in your honor. You really do owe it to your fans and supporters to let them get a good look at you."

At that very moment, a woman approached them, armed with a gold Cross pen and cocktail napkin. "Dear Miss Jefferson," she said in a high-pitched voice, tinged with an elite Boston accent, "would you let me have your autograph? I just know you'll be famous in a few years, and I would like to be able to say, 'I knew her when . . .'" The stranger extended her heavily jewelled hand towards Anne. Anne took the napkin from her, looked up at Greg, and saw him trying to control his laughter. She signed the napkin. "Thank you, my dear," the lady said as she walked away, waving victoriously. As soon as she was out of range, Greg cracked up.

"Quiet! She'll hear you," Anne said, about to laugh herself.

"My dear Miss Jefferson," Greg said, perfectly imitating the autograph hound's shrill voice, "would you let me get you some punch. I want to be able to say, 'I fed her when!'"

The rest of the evening was perfect. Anne

and Greg satisfied themselves with food and drink, danced endlessly and talked about everything under the sun. They even managed to get four seats together at the same table, so that when Anne's parents arrived, Greg and they got to know each other better.

"Well, Cinderella, how do you like your ball?" Mr. Jefferson asked.

Anne was embarrassed. She hadn't wanted her Cinderella fantasy to be advertised outside of the apartment. "Honestly, Dad, that private joke was not for publication," she stammered. She felt the color rising to her cheeks, and she turned away from Greg, afraid he must think she was very childish.

Greg was reassuring. "Hey, Annie, don't worry about it for a second. If you're Cinderella, that makes me Prince Charming. I can't hate that. It certainly beats being the big, bad wolf." Everyone at the table laughed.

"However," Mrs. Jefferson added, "that makes me the wicked stepmother, and I'm not at all sure I'm suited for the role."

"Well," Mr. Jefferson said, "as long as you promise not to rush out of here the way you rushed out of the club, and as long as you manage to keep both shoes on your feet all the way home, I think the rest of us can muddle through this just fine."

"Anne," Greg said after the laughter had died down, "they're playing our song." He led her to the dance floor. The music was slow and romantic, and Greg wrapped his arms around her and moved to the melody. Anne couldn't help smiling as she listened to him humming in her ear.

"If this is going to be 'our song,' " she said, "I think I have a right to know what it is."

"It's called 'What I Did For Love.' It's from *A Chorus Line*, the big Broadway hit."

How appropriate, Anne thought to herself. She wondered if Greg had any idea what she had done for his love, and how good she felt now that she was sure of it. As she moved her body closer to his and swayed to the music, her thoughts drifted back to those first days in New York City. What a child she had been then—a mixed-up kid, ready for something to happen, anxious for it to happen, but not exactly sure what was going to happen. And when it finally did start happening, she let herself get lost trying to force it to happen her way. Still, somehow, it all came out all right.

She looked up into Greg's eyes. "I'm so happy," she said. "I'm so glad to be here with you. You have no idea what this night means to me."

"I'm glad, Annie. I'm glad you've gotten over your hurt about not coming in first in the finals."

"I came in first where it counted. I'm dancing with you, right?"

"And is that all you really cared about? I still can't believe that."

"Greg, you have to remember what things were like for me at the beginning. I had just arrived in Manhattan from Maine. I felt totally unsophisticated and very insecure. Then I saw you. Then I saw Sarah. Then I took a good look at myself and came up short. I felt as if I had to prove something to myself, to you, even to Sarah. It had nothing to do with the way you acted. And Sarah was always as nice as she could be. I see that now. No, I can't blame anyone but myself."

"But that's all behind you now, Anne," Greg said, sensing a sadness coming back into Anne's mood. "You did what you thought was best, and it all worked out in the end. Let's talk about something else."

The subject was dropped, and the dancing continued happily. Anne and Greg finally returned to their table only after the orchestra took a break. A few moments later, the lights dimmed and the musicians struck up a fanfare.

"Ladies and Gentlemen, may I have your attention please." Mr. Tompkins had taken over the microphone in front of the band. He looked different in a tuxedo, Anne thought, stiffer and less comfortable. "It is time for our awards presentation to begin." Chairs shuffled into position, and glasses clinked down on the tables. "I think you all will agree," Mr. Tompkins contin-

143

ued after the room quieted down, "that this year's competition was perhaps the finest ever held by the Metropolitan Gymnastics Club and that everyone in it deserves a round of applause." The audience obliged. "We have watched some familiar faces and met some new faces this year." Greg turned around and nudged Anne proudly. "And I, for one, am very proud of the way they all performed. Now, on to the presentation."

First came the men's awards. Anne clapped fiercely as Greg was handed his individual medal, and she gave him a big kiss when he returned to the table. More applause followed as the other male winners came up to claim their prizes.

Finally, it was the women's turn. Jennifer Cornell was asked to come up first to receive her bronze medal for her third-place finish in the all-around competition. The wait was endless for Anne. Her knees were shaking and her heart pounding as Mr. Tompkins took the microphone in his hands after the applause had died down.

"Before presenting this next award," he said, excruciatingly slowly, "I would like to say a few words about our second-place finisher and winner of the individual balance beam title." Anne could feel the sweat trickling down her back. She wanted this to be over. "Anne Jefferson came to us about four months ago with very little gymnastics training. She never had been in a real competition before this one. She worked harder than I've ever seen anyone work, and

144

she achieved more in that amount of time than even I thought possible. She has been a shining example of devotion and dedication and determination, and she is a welcome addition to our family. I am proud to have worked with her. The winner of this year's individual balance beam award and our second-place all-around finisher is Anne Jefferson."

The crowd broke into applause and cheers. As Anne walked up to the podium, she saw Greg standing and clapping, and she was astounded to see other people getting up to give her a standing ovation. She was beaming. As she carefully wove her way through the tables and mounted the platform, she realized that she had never been happier in her whole life. She took the two medals in her hands, showed them to the audience, shook hands with Mr. Tompkins, and moved to the back of the stage. Jennifer congratulated her, and they stood there together, awkward and self-conscious, until the frenzy died down and people took their seats.

"Now, for our champion. She needs little introduction. She's been here many times before. Ladies and Gentlemen, Sarah Bartos." Once again, the crowd cheered. Sarah glided up to the platform and accepted her awards graciously. She came over to Anne and Jennifer and congratulated them, too. Then they all took each other's hands and held them up in a victory pose. Cameras flashed. The lights in the room came on full again. Mr. Tompkins announced the end of the ceremony and suggested that everyone continue their dancing and fun. It was over. Greg rushed up to the stage and grabbed Anne's hand. "I'm so proud of you," he said, pulling her away.

"Hold on a second, little brother. Remember me?" Sarah said. Anne couldn't help smiling. How many times had she felt the same way? How many times had she wished she were in Sarah's place, getting all the attention and praise. Well, it felt good, darned good, to have them at last.

"The face is familiar," Greg kidded. "Oh, yeah, I remember now. Hello Sis."

"Never mind the humor," Sarah said. "I'd like to borrow Anne for a few minutes, if you can bear to let her out of your sight. You don't mind, do you Anne?"

"Not at all."

Greg shrugged. "OK, I can't argue. But I have my watch on, and if you don't bring her back soon, I'll sick the Dobermans on you."

"Your unwavering family devotion is touching," Sarah said facetiously. "I'll have her back to you soon. Calm down."

Greg could see that Anne was becoming uncomfortable. "I'll be right here waiting," he said, trying to assure her that everything would be all right.

Sarah led Anne out of the ballroom and

down the hall, away from the music and chatter. They both took seats on a small antique couch. Anne was unreasonably nervous, and she waited anxiously to find out what all this was about.

"I don't know if this is the time or the place," Sarah said at last, "but I have a few things I want to say to you, and I had to grab the opportunity while I had it. First of all, I wanted to tell you that you were terrific today. You really had me scared there for a while. I was amazed and pleased at the progress you've made, and I'd like to ask you to help me train for the Olympics. I know I still have a long way to go, but I feel that I could learn a lot from you, if you'd let me. You have a winning spirit about you that, I'm hoping, is contagious." Anne sat dumbfounded as Sarah spoke. She couldn't believe her ears. "Will you help me, Anne?" Anne managed an affirmative nod.

"Thank you," Sarah said. "And while I'm thanking you, thank you for what you've done to Greg."

"What do you mean?" Anne asked, baffled.

"Come on, Anne. Surely you see how much he's changed? I love Greg. I want you to understand that. But he was becoming a royal pain to me. All he seemed to care about was helping me become a champion. He never seemed to have a life of his own. But you changed all that. He sort of lit up the first time he saw you, and he's been shining ever since. He's crazy about you, you know, and I've never been happier. Before he met you, he was much too serious. He studied all the time or sat in his room reading or followed me around. Now he goes out and has fun, he talks about nothing but you at home, and he's come alive. You're wonderful for him . . . and for me. You're a very special girl, Anne."

"Sarah," Anne said, not sure if she should go on. "I owe you an apology. This is very hard for me to admit, but ever since I met Greg, I've been jealous of you and hostile towards you for no good reason at all. This has never happened to me before, but I forced myself to dislike you without even knowing you. I let myself make foolish snap judgments. I thought you were my rival for Greg's attention, and from the beginning I set my sights on putting you down in some way. It was wrong, very wrong, and I wanted to let you know how sorry I am. You're a good person, Sarah, and I want you to be a good friend."

"You can count on that, Anne. I felt some of your hostility, but I figured it had to do with the competition. Now that I think about it, it's easy to see how Greg's attitude toward me could be threatening to another girl. I only considered the problems it was causing *me*, not how it made you feel. I'm really sorry about all that, but at least it seems to have worked out well."

She smiled at Anne. "I'd better get you back to Greg."

Greg was pacing back and forth at the other end of the hall, obviously worried about what was taking so long. "Here we are, Greg," Sarah said when they spotted each other. "And there's not a scratch on her."

"See you later, Sarah," Anne said as she and Greg started back to their table.

"I'll see you at the club Saturday," Sarah said, heading for the dance floor with her date.

"What was all that about?" Greg asked, bewildered. "Did she tell you all the family secrets?"

Anne grinned. "Do you have something to hide?"

"Certainly not. Don't tease me, Annie. I was really worried about you, knowing how you feel about my sister and all."

"Well, you can stop worrying. I think Sarah is one of the nicest people I know."

"Boy am I confused," Greg said, putting his hand across his brow. "But it's great that you've changed your mind about Sarah."

"I've changed my mind about a lot of things. I sure have learned a lot in one day."

"Care to elaborate on that deep, psychological statement?"

"If you're interested."

"I am. Really."

"OK. I learned that your sister is about as

special as they come, that she is everything you said she was and more. I learned that I'm not such a bad person myself. I've learned the importance of being a winner . . . and I've learned the true definition of being a winner. And speaking of winners, Merry Christmas." Anne handed Greg the leather case containing her silver medal. "It isn't exactly what I planned, but they were out of the right color. Still, I think you know it comes from the heart."

"Annie, I can't take this. You worked so hard for it."

"I want you to have it, Greg. I really do."

Greg took the box reluctantly. He stared at it for a long eternity. "Anne," he said, looking up at her, "I love you. I'll treasure this forever."

"And I'll treasure this forever," she said, holding out the ring he had given her.

As Greg leaned over and kissed her tenderly, Anne closed her eyes and savored this, the most perfect moment in her life. And as she melted in the arms of her first prize, she felt like the true winner she had finally become. She had won Greg, she had won Sarah's friendship, and she had won back her own self-respect and confidence. For these, after all, were the victories that really counted.

Sweet Dreams Diary ™

(01456-0) 5¼" × 7⅝" $5.95

Now you can have a place to record all your dreams, secret desires and special feelings. The SWEET DREAMS DIARY gives you the perfect opportunity to jot it all down. Plus, it's filled with sayings about love and friendship, poems, and astrological information. The diary is spiral-bound, which makes it easy to write in, no matter where you are.

So order your copy of the SWEET DREAMS DIARY today—and let your friends know about it. In the years to come, you'll be able to look back in your diary and see which of your dreams have come true!

— — — — — — — — — — — — — — — —

Read these great new <u>Sweet Dreams</u> romances on sale soon:

☐ #23 FALLING IN LOVE AGAIN
by Barbara Conklin
(On sale September 15 · #22840-4 · $1.95)

Mariah's not one of those girls who's never been kissed. She had a boyfriend. Once. But Paul died, and Mariah thinks she'll never find anyone as special again. So when Dan asks her out, Mariah doesn't know what to think. He's sweet and funny and understanding—but Paul's memory always seems to be between them. Now Mariah knows she must choose—between Dan who loves her now, and Paul who loved her first...

☐ #24 THE TROUBLE WITH CHARLIE *by Joan Lowery Nixon*
(On sale September 15 · #22957-5 · $1.95)

Here's Charlie. She has two big brothers so her dating life must be terrific. Right? Wrong! Her brothers act like watchdogs everywhere she goes and all the best guys have been scared off. Now only the wrong guys ask her out. Charlie's about to give up altogether. Boy, has she got boy trouble!

☐ #25 HER SECRET SELF
by Rhondi Villot
(On sale October 15 · #22543-X · $1.95)

Joanne enjoys doing impressions of famous people, but her impersonations are making her miserable. Even her boyfriend has gotten tired of her role-playing and has started dating gorgeous Christiana. Then Joanne meets Cliff, the class president, and he seems really interested in her—until he is stung by one of her imitations. Will Joanne's illusions keep her from ever finding real-life happiness?

☐ #26 THIS MUST BE MAGIC
by Marian Woodruff
(On sale October 15 · #22692-4 · $1.95)

It's the junior class genie week and Kerrie's friends have gotten together to buy her dreamy Mike in the genie auction. Working together with Mike in hopes of winning awards for best couple, best stunts and best costume at the school parade at the end of the week, Kerrie realizes just how much she has been missing paying so much attention to school work and not enough to boys. But can she ever possibly hope to lure Mike away from his beautiful girlfriend Marcy?

Buy these books at your local bookstore or use this handy coupon for ordering:

You'll fall in love with all the Sweet Dreams romances. Reading these stories, you'll be reminded of yourself or of someone you know. There's Jennie, the *California Girl*, who becomes an outsider when her family moves to Texas. And Cindy, the *Little Sister*, who's afraid that Christine, the oldest in the family, will steal her new boyfriend. Don't miss any of the Sweet Dreams romances.

☐	14019	**P.S. I LOVE YOU** Barbara P. Conklin	$1.95
☐	20325	**THE POPULARITY PLAN** Rosemary Vernon	$1.75
☐	20327	**LAURIE'S SONG** Debra Brand	$1.75
☐	14020	**PRINCESS AMY** Melinda Pollowitz	$1.95
☐	20326	**LITTLE SISTER** Yvonne Green	$1.75
☐	20324	**CALIFORNIA GIRL** Janet Quin-Harkin	$1.75
☐	14022	**GREEN EYES** Suzanne Rand	$1.95
☐	14021	**THE THOROUGHBRED** Joanna Campbell	$1.95
☐	22991	**COVER GIRL** Yvonne Green	$1.95
☐	22992	**LOVE MATCH** Janet Quin-Harkin	$1.95
☐	20787	**THE PROBLEM WITH LOVE** Susan Mendonca	$1.75
☐	20788	**NIGHT OF THE PROM** Debra Spector	$1.75
☐	22607	**ALL'S FAIR IN LOVE** Jeanne Andrews	$1.95
☐	22683	**SECRET IDENTITY** Joanna Campbell	$1.95

Buy them at your local bookstore or use this handy coupon for ordering: